In His Steps:
THE
PROMISE

Joey O'Connor is the director of the Orange County Grief Recovery Outreach Program and the author of ten books for couples, parents, and young adults. His book *Heaven's Not a Crying Place: Teaching Your Child about Funerals, Death, and the Life Beyond* was awarded the 1998 California Funeral Directors' Association Media Award. He lives with his wife and children in San Clemente, California.

His works include:

Breaking Your Comfort Zones: And 49 Extremely Radical Ways to Live for God
Excuse Me! I'll Take My Piece of the Planet Now
Graffiti for Girls by J. David Schmidt with Joey O'Connor
Graffiti for Guys by J. David Schmidt with Joey O'Connor
Heaven's Not a Crying Place: Teaching Your Child about Funerals, Death, and the Life Beyond
Whadd'ya Gonna Do? 25 Steps for Getting a Life
Where Is God When . . . 1001 Answers to Questions Students Are Asking
Women Are Always Right & Men Are Never Wrong: Finding Common Ground in Your Marriage without Going to Extremes
You're Grounded for Life! And 49 Other Crazy Things Parents Say

For speaking events, conferences and seminars, please call (949) 369-6767. You can also write to Joey O'Connor at P.O. Box 3373, San Clemente, CA 92674-3373.

For more information about Joey O'Connor's books and the Orange County Grief Recovery Outreach Program, visit Joey's web site: http://www.joeyo.com. You can email Joey with your comments and questions at: joey@joeyo.com

In His Steps:
THE
PROMISE

JOEY O'CONNOR

Fleming H. Revell
A Division of Baker Book House
Grand Rapids, Michigan 49516

Published by Fleming H. Revell
a division of Baker Book House Company
P.O. Box 6287, Grand Rapids, MI 49516-6287

Printed in the United States of America

Library of Congress Cataloging-in-Publication Data

O'Connor, Joey, 1964–
  In his steps : the promise / Joey O'Connor
     p.   cm.
  ISBN 0-8007-5678-9 (pbk.)
  I. Title.
  PS3565.C612I52   1998
  813'.54—dc21   98-40721

For current information about all releases from Baker Book House, visit our web site:
http://www.bakerbooks.com

This book is dedicated to the glory of God
and to a man whose life reflects that image,
Bill Petersen

1

everend Max Henry! It's Friday afternoon; I thought you came home to finish your sermon," Kate Henry mocked in disbelief as she caught her husband, toothbrush and chrome cleaner in hand, leaning over the handlebars of his cherry-red Harley Davidson motorcycle.

"I did, hon. I'm just taking a break. You can't believe how many interruptions I had today at the office; everyone wanted a piece of me! Hey, hand me that rag, would you, please?"

Kate picked up a frayed, yellow cloth from the driveway of their family's two-story in the historic Highland district of the city known for rose parades and college bowl games. Taking aim, she nailed the pastor of Pasadena's First Church with a direct hit to the face.

"Hey, watch it! With all the distractions I've had today, I'm ready to call in sick on Sunday. Besides, I'll have you know that there is a distinct link to polishing a Harley and polishing a sermon. As I work on one, I am also mentally working on the other."

"Gimme a break." Kate laughed as she straddled the bike and asked about the topic of his upcoming message.

"Following in the steps of Jesus," Max started. "There's a verse in 1 Peter that talks about how we should follow in his steps because he suffered for us. I've already found a couple perfect quotes in *Time* magazine. I've got the four main points outlined, but I'm struggling to come up with a creative closing to show the congregation how to really follow Christ. I mean, I love working at First Church, but how many pastors have to speak to a congregation like ours?"

"You're right, dear," Kate said sarcastically. "You have a terribly difficult job with all that ministry that happens on Annandale Golf Course, an annual budget that's been in the black for the past seven years, free Rose Bowl passes, and five weeks' vacation every year. Yes, yours is a treacherous calling—ministering to the wealthy and wise of Pasadena's finest. Not to mention our upcoming trip to Paris this summer . . ."

"Okay, enough already. I wave the white, er, yellow flag." Max laughed as he spun the tattered rag over his head. "Don't you have anything better to do than pick on a biker preacher?"

"As a matter of fact, I do. I'm heading over to the preschool to see what supplies we need for next week. It's already four-fifteen, so I need to get going. There's a fresh pot of coffee for you." Kate leaned over the handlebars and gave her husband a warm kiss good-bye.

"Thanks, dear. I'll see you in a few hours or so." Max waved as he gave the silvery chrome a final swipe and stood back to admire the clean lines of the beautiful highway hog he had received as a surprise birthday present the year before from the members of First Church.

Max had always wanted a Harley but never knew how he could buy one without inciting a flurry of church gossip about the senior pastor cruising Colorado Boulevard and rattling upscale shops with the deafening belch of his roaring Harley. The fact that the motorcycle had been a gift gave Max the perfect out. Vic Gennaro, owner of a nationwide chain of leather stores and a prominent member of First Church, had even had a custom leather jacket designed to match the cycle's silver-studded saddlebags. Emblazoned on the back of the black jacket in bold red letters was the proud title, *F.C. Pastor*.

It had been eight years since Max had risen to the leadership helm as senior pastor of Pasadena's oldest and most respected church. The members of First Church admired this good-looking pastor with the keen intellect, playful sense of humor, and articulate speaking skills. Max's position at First Church was known by those in ministry as "a good gig."

A gifted communicator, Max knew how to blend timeless biblical principles with inspirational stories and practical steps for his congregation. His real-life stories appealed to the hearts of his people, and because those stories weren't of the touchy-feely variety, his words weren't reduced to sappy spiritual drivel. His use of humor, relevant examples of local and world events, intellectual curiosity, and remarkable lack of religious pomposity made him easy to listen to as a pastor and easy to like as a person. A couple strong-selling books on motivation and the life of Christ made him a sought-after speaker at corporate and religious conferences across the country.

At thirty-nine years old, Max garnered a base salary of sixty grand a year plus annual book royalties that averaged an additional fifty thousand. Max tried to limit his travel schedule outside of California, but he and Kate managed to capture the four seasons by escaping to the local mountain communities of Big Bear and Lake Arrowhead, where Max spoke at Christian camps and retreats. Throw in some hefty speaking fees and Max's annual income was well past six-figures; but the real clincher was the little known gift from the IRS in the form of the minister's housing allowance and personal exemption from Social Security tax. Max couldn't remember the last time he had paid federal or state income taxes. His accountant, under every provision legally entitled to Max by U.S. law, helped him capitalize on the benefits afforded to all ministers. It was Max's job, though, to keep a thorough record of his housing expenses and royalty receipts. Max had a good thing going, and he knew it. He couldn't complain. First Church *was* a good gig.

Despite a comfortable living and his growing national influence as a Christian personality, Max quietly struggled with the reality that he and Kate were unable to bear children. For years, Kate had suffered from endometriosis. Surgery after surgery offered the hope of someday having a child all their own, but the final results only yielded disappointment and questions of unanswered prayers. Three failed attempts at in vitro fertilization cost Kate and Max thousands of dollars but also more than enough heartbreak to erode their collective will to try again. Max had tried to bring up the subject of adoption, but Kate wouldn't hear a word of it. The inner wounds were still too fresh. She said she just wasn't ready.

Throwing the rag on the Harley, Max walked to the back door of the house. Though working on his bike was a needed break, he was anxious to get upstairs and finish his sermon. Not known for patience when pressed for time, Max was glad he'd have the next couple hours to himself. He was halfway up the stairs when the doorbell rang.

Before the front door was fully ajar, a rancid odor hit Max's nostrils with a repulsive punch. Wearing a red *Quick-Print* cap, a young, unshaven man stood before him in a baggy sweatshirt, dirty Levi's with holes in the knees, and muddy leather shoes. He was the kind of person Max had often seen on street corners in South Pasadena or in front of supermarkets bumming spare change or, even occasionally, lying asleep on the sidewalk on Lake Street after a long night's binge. Max wasn't used to interacting with homeless people. It was a whole other world he didn't understand. Nor was he sure he ever really wanted to understand. As he looked at the tired, weary face of the young man, Max couldn't help but feel sorry for him. Still, he did have his sermon to finish. Before Max knew what to make of what was sure to be an unusual conversation, the young man said humbly, "Excuse me, sir. Are you Max Henry, the pastor of First Church? I'm sorry to bother you at home, but I need your help."

Max hesitated, then replied, "Well, yes . . . I'm Max. What can I do for you?"

The man was ready to get right to his point, but before he could do so, he let out a violent hack that launched an uncontrollable coughing spasm. He bent over, hands on knees, trying to catch his breath and slow the attack.

Max stood there feeling uncomfortable, not sure what to do.

Finally, the young man stood up, wiped a yellowish drool from his chin, and said, "I was told you could help me find a job. I'm outta work, and I hear that there's a lot of people in your church who own companies and factories. Stores, odd jobs, yard work; I'll take anything I can get. I'm desperate."

Max felt torn. Part of him was saying, "I don't have time for this." The other half of him pleaded compassion and patience. He thought about his limited options for truly helping the man. He reasoned a moment and said to the stranger, "I'm sorry, but our church doesn't have that kind of ministry. We fund a mission downtown that's better equipped to help you. I wish I could help you, but I honestly don't get requests like this very often."

Pulling the cap off his head, the man held it with both hands and said, "Sir, you don't understand. I was sent to you by another church. They said you—your church, that is—has the resources or at least connections to be able to help me. I've already been to four or five churches, and they keep bouncing me around from church to church. 'First Church,' they said. 'Go to First Church. If there's anyone who can help, it's First Church.'"

Max got an idea, eased a bit, and said, "Listen, I really think your best bet is to go down to the mission. See if they can help you. If not, come by my office on Monday." Fishing around in his pants pocket, he pulled out a wrinkled ten-dollar bill. "Here; take this. At least you'll be able to get something to eat. I'm sorry; I wish I could be of more help, but I'm terribly busy right now. Maybe we can talk on Monday?" Max's voice trailed off as he slowly shut his white, lacquered front door.

The stranger stood on the front porch fingering the bill. He shook his head, stuffed the cash in his pocket, and slowly walked away.

Max looked out the front window from behind the drapes as the man headed down the sidewalk with his head hanging low. Max shook his head, subconsciously releasing the tension from his conversation with the surprise visitor. He turned around and started up the stairs to his study to finish his sermon. He'd had enough interruptions for one day and hated the thought of working on Saturday. Kate would be home soon, and he wanted his sermon printed out before they left for their favorite Italian restaurant.

On Saturday night, after six, Rikki Winslow and her mother, Valerie, were still at White Dove Recording Studios. From the loudspeakers came the voice of a man sitting in a glass-enclosed booth before a large control panel filled with hundreds of knobs, "Okay, Rikki, let's try the chorus one more time with a little more emphasis on the last word of each verse. I know it's been a long day, but we gotta get this right. Ya still with me?"

The teenage girl sitting on a leather stool wearing headphones nodded and replied, "Sound's great. Let's do it again."

The sound engineer ran the tape again, an acoustic guitar ballad with a soft beat. In a vibrant, earthy voice that was as pure as mountain air, the girl began to sing, her voice without pretense or conceit. The engineers in the booth nodded, smiled at each other, and gently rocked to the easy rhythm.

Meanwhile, hunched over a messy desk in the far corner of the booth, a petite, middle-aged woman with mousey, primped hair and long, red fingernails rasped demands into a telephone.

"Listen, Dean, we've been working on this contract for two months now, and as you can tell, I'm getting a bit impatient. Here it is, Saturday night. We're making you another demo tape and you have nothing for us. Everybody's already listened to the other tapes, you've showcased her in front of eight recording labels, five of which made immediate offers, and now you're telling me it's up to Rikki to decide what label she wants to sing on? I'm the mother here, and she is still a minor. It is *your* job to recommend to *me* the top two companies for *me* to choose for *her!* What do you think I hired you for?"

Clicking her fingernails on the metal desk, Valerie Winslow rolled her eyes as she leaned back in the chair and listened to a slew of pathetic excuses for why she didn't have a signed recording contract in hand. "Listen; all I have to say is that we'd better be recording by July or you'll be out of a job. Rikki graduates in June, and she's too busy with school and church to start any earlier. We are leaving our entire summer open to do this album. When she starts, I want her completely focused. That means all business matters and concert schedules need to be set beforehand. Do we have a clear understanding on this?"

Valerie eased back, the corners of her mouth turned up as she reveled in the agent's profuse apologies. Yes, promises on his mother's grave. And yes, Valerie, assurances of a lucrative contract.

Coming about, Valerie plied in a silky voice, "By the way, Dean, did Foundation Records meet our counter of a hundred grand?" The staccato of her nails on the desk increased. "Good. That's very good, Dean. Listen, I've got to get going now. It's late, and Rikki and I have church in the morning. You call me when you have the best two offers for me to choose from, okay, dear? Bye now." Finally, with a satisfied smile on her face, Valerie turned to the studio to watch Rikki finish the take.

On Sunday morning the January air had a crisp snap to it as expensive cars began to fill First Church's parking lot. The gentle ridgelines of the nearby San Gabriel mountains framed this picture-perfect day, the kind of day that makes Southern California the envy of the rest of the nation. Mothers and fathers with children in tow, elderly couples, and single professionals got out of their cars, making their way to the main building—the adults to the sanctuary and the children to their Sunday school classes.

First Church wasn't a large church, yet it boasted a few hundred members of Pasadena's wealthiest and most prominent families. The older adults, chiseled with experience and wisdom, were refined and intellectual. Doctors, lawyers, executives of Fortune 500 firms, entrepreneurs of companies with gazelle-like success, and scientists from Jet Propulsion Laboratory and the California Institute of

Technology filled the pews along with their wives, who, if they weren't doctors, lawyers, or executives themselves, were active in cotillion programs, Rose Parade committees, and Charity League events. First Church was a dynamic combination of old wealth and young energy. The younger professionals were smart, driven, and networked. Because of the high cost of living in the nicer areas of Pasadena, most young families in the congregation were two-income households with children either in day care or left at home with a nanny.

First Church could have been Any Church, USA. Except for the economic demographics of its members, First Church had its share of true believers as well as its skeptics and those who were quietly unconvinced. There were people of faith and people who faked. Many wanted to know and please God; still others were there for show, making a nominal profession of faith limited to Sunday mornings. Some members attended out of a sense of moral obligation and a need for self-improvement not rooted in an authentic spirituality but more along the lines of improving their first-serve percentage or putting stroke. Like any other church, there was a contingent of members who considered religion an intensely personal and private affair, which made it convenient to keep others at a safe distance. Still, many First Church members daily lived out their trust in Christ. Faithful. Determined. Dependent on grace. Rich in compassion and mercy. Not perfect as humans but persevering in spirit. It was these individuals who were able to look past the trappings of their culture and the shortcomings of their church, even though they still struggled with the temptation to conform to society's standards and complain about how God's church was supposed to be.

Like many of the nearby country clubs, to some First Church had an air of exclusivity and an almost diplomatic reserve. Though the congregation did like a thoughtful sermon filled with good jokes and inspiring, heartwarming stories, there was still a certain stiffness to the service. Worship was ordered, specific, and controlled. They never deviated from the regular order of service, preferring a stable and predictable experience each week, except for when they wheeled that Harley straight down the center aisle on Max's thirty-eighth birthday.

First Church resisted popular worship trends of guitar solos, drums, electronic synthesizers, and big screen monitors. Instead, the members prided themselves on a worship style they felt expressed a quiet and reflective reverence for the Almighty. Accordingly, First Church's music program was the best in the city. Without regard to expense, First Church employed the best choir director and professional musicians to instill a sense of grandeur in worship. Sponsoring an annual calendar filled with classical concerts and community events, the First Church music program was well known throughout Pasadena and the surrounding communities for its contribution to the arts.

The service began, and just before the sermon, Rikki Winslow stood before the congregation and sang a mesmerizing arrangement of the hymn "I Surrender All." Max relaxed in his chair as Rikki's young, vibrant voice soothed the subtle uneasiness he always felt moments before he preached. He liked having music before he preached, knowing that a good song made the congregation more receptive to his message.

Rikki ended the song with a powerful display of poise and clarity, her vocal strength as compelling as her beauty. The congregation offered a polite round of applause no louder than that at a golf tournament, but with sincere appreciation for Rikki's artistry. More than a few members admitted to each other that First Church's music program was why they attended, and Rikki's weekly contribution played no small part in their decision.

Pastor Max adjusted his lapel microphone and rose to his understated, yet elegant pulpit. Within minutes, he had his rhythm. Max quoted from the words of Jesus, offered a modern-day illustration of Bill Gates memorizing the whole Sermon on the Mount as a teenager, put the congregation into stitches about a silly fight he and Kate had had a week earlier, and finally, held up copies of *Time* and *Wired* magazines and declared, "*Time* magazine says we're 'wired and tired.' I think they're right. We are anxious. Distressed. Discouraged. How can we follow Jesus when we can barely lift our heads out of bed on Saturday morning?"

It was no secret that Pastor Max loved to preach, and the members of First Church prided themselves on having such a gifted, articulate pastor whose national reputation was growing through his book and tape sales. They appreciated his efforts to make his messages contemporary.

If only First Church members knew how much time Max spent in sermon preparation. At the beginning of the week, his desk was clean. By Thursday though, it was littered with resources of all kinds: clippings from the *Los Angeles Times* sports page, articles from *Inc.*, *Fortune*, and *Newsweek* magazines, the latest works by notable Christian authors, cartoons with funny punch lines, biblical commentaries, the latest motivational and management books, Greek and Hebrew lexicons, yellow legal pads filled with scribbled notes, stacks of CD-ROM's, and a long list of items for his secretary to research on the Internet. His worn, brown leather Bible competed with all these items for space on the large desk in his First Church office.

Max knew how to deliver a message with impact. He had studied the secrets of the greatest motivational speakers of the past twenty years and often spoke in quiet, hushed tones before—*wham*—he executed his main point like an ax striking a tree. Understanding the power of nonverbal communication, Max used body language to draw even the tiredest eyes in his direction. Sweep arms. Fold hands. Scratch head. Lean on pulpit. Put hands on hips. He occasionally even stepped out from behind the pulpit and went down on one knee like a 1950s soap salesman begging a poor housewife to let him show his wares. Anything for a sale.

The only thing that distracted him was a poor turnout. Southern Californians were weather wimps. They were as noncommittal for showing up to church as they were for their professional sports teams. Max always read the three-to five-day forecasts early in the week to gauge what Sunday's attendance would be like. His mood on Sunday was largely dependent on the size of the congregation. A small service and Max felt painfully self-conscious.

But with beautiful weather and a packed house like today, Max was passionate, bold, confident, enthusiastic, and authoritative. He was in clear command of his subject and audience. Max's handsome face and rich voice drew every head forward as he leaned on the pulpit and concluded his sermon with four simple steps for following Jesus.

"To wrap up our final message in this series, Following in His Steps, the four things we have looked at today are learning to love, taking steps of faith, obeying God's Word, and imitating the life of Christ. Do these four things and it will go well with you as you honor God and love your neighbor."

It was a good message. Funny. Relevant. Inspirational and biblical. But something was lacking, and more than a few First Church members quietly asked themselves, "So what? How am I supposed to live that way in the real world?"

Just as Max finished the closing prayer and the choir rose to sing a final hymn, a noisy commotion erupted in the back of the church with the shout of a man's voice. In unison, hundreds of worshippers lurched around to see who was initiating this unprecedented break of First Church protocol. Headed straight down the green carpet in the center aisle, his smell preceding him, was a scraggly dressed vagrant wearing a red baseball cap. When he reached the front of the church, the man turned and faced the congregation.

"Don't worry, I'm not drunk or on drugs, and I won't harm anyone," the man began in a scratchy voice, slipping his hat off his head. "I'd just like to say my piece and ask you a few questions about the sermon we all just heard. At the rate I'm going, I'll probably be dead soon, so I'd like to get some things off my chest that have been bothering me the past couple weeks."

Max rose from his chair in complete astonishment and walked toward the pulpit. His eyes zeroed in on the man's red hat: *QuickPrint*. It was the same young man who had knocked on his door two days ago—same dirty sweatshirt, Levi's, and leather shoes now minus the mud. Still unshaven, he looked tired and sickly. His thin, gaunt face had round, dark circles under the eyes like twin caves. His greasy, matted hair was flat and sticky looking where the hat had rested. He nervously shifted back and forth and looked up at Max for some sort of permission to begin.

Making swift, deliberate steps down the side aisles, four ushers in suits and ties almost reached the young vagrant before Max waved them back with a furtive gesture. Max nodded to the young man and held his hands forward in a reassuring gesture toward the congregation.

The man didn't look agitated or excited, like he was ready to mow down the congregation with a machine gun or spew a mouthful of obscenities. He was calm, oblivious that he had stepped across an unseen, unspoken line. His words were slow. Intentional. A few members thought about rising to drag this bum back to the street from where he came, but bowed to Max's leadership. Others, who had seen this man standing outside before the service began, felt sorry for him and wondered what had led up to his physical deterioration. A number of church members prayed silently for the man, but overall, a changed atmosphere of restraint kept everyone in their seats. Nervous laughter sneaked out of a few mouths, but most everyone held their breath like a crowd of beachgoers getting ready to dive under a huge, unexpected wave.

As the man spoke, Max didn't do anything but lean against the pulpit with a look of sadness and resignation on his face. The best thing to do, he thought, was to give the poor guy a few minutes, thank him for visiting First Church and for what he had to say, then let him go on his way. Rikki Winslow, however, was intrigued. She pulled her long, brown hair over one shoulder and leaned forward in rapt anticipation. Her soft, olive-colored skin and captivating, emerald eyes radiated a warm compassion.

"I know I shouldn't come into such a fine church like this dressed the way I am, but I haven't always looked this bad. I know what most of you are probably thinking, but I'm not a beggar. Homeless, yes, but not by choice." The man spoke in a natural and honest voice. He addressed the crowd in a humble yet confident way, as if he thought they might benefit by what he was going to say.

"I'm a printer by trade. In fact, just a year ago, I owned my own franchise, but when the company went belly-up, so did I. With all the corporate downsizing going on and the competitiveness in the marketplace, it's been pretty tough to get a job. I'm not complaining. I'm just telling it the way it is. With how expensive it is to live today, it seems that just about every family is three months away from homelessness. Lose your job. Get racked up in credit debt and medical bills. Miss a mortgage payment, then another. It's a slow, nasty spiral down the drain. I've been in three states looking for a new job and have nothing to show for it. Then I figured, I'll go to California. There's plenty of work there, the weather's nice, people are friendly . . . or so I thought . . . the weather, that is."

The man put his hand to his mouth and let forth a virulent hack. The congregation winced at the sound. "But I was wondering, as I sat here in church this morning, if what you call following Jesus is the same thing as what he taught. What did he mean when he said, 'Follow me'?"

He gestured at Max and continued. "Your pastor said that it was necessary for the disciple of Jesus to follow his steps, and he said the steps were obedience, faith, love, and imitation. The message had a nice delivery and all—'bout the best I've ever seen—but I didn't hear him go into a lot of detail about that last step. What do Christians today do to follow in the steps of Jesus?

"I've been in Pasadena for two weeks looking for work, and in all that time I haven't received a word of comfort or encouragement except from your minister here, who said he was sorry and gave me ten bucks for a meal. No, when your car breaks down, and you don't have any money, and you're living on the streets for over a week, it doesn't take long to look like roadkill. I've spent my days trying to find any sort of odd job that I can and my nights sleeping under bridges. I'm not blaming anybody, am I? I'm just stating facts.

"Just a year ago I was happily married with a great wife and a young daughter. I won't bother you with how my wife died four months ago, but I know the one thing that broke her heart was losing our home. It had a nice little backyard for our daughter to play in. Seems that the banker who foreclosed on our home went to a church right down the street from us. As I sat listening to her singing," he paused and looked at Rikki, "I wondered if he surrendered all to follow Jesus? Anyway, my daughter has been living with relatives while I've been looking for a job. She's lost her mother and I can't provide for her. Then I come here and I get confused when I see so many Christians living in luxury and singing all kinds of songs about following him, all the while there's people like me willing to work hard if someone would only give 'em a break.

"Of course, I understand that you are busy people with problems and struggles and frustrations of your own, so I don't expect you to stop everything you're doing to find me a job. But, what I'm struggling with here is, what is meant by following Jesus? What do you mean when you sing, 'I surrender all; I surrender all.' Do you really mean 'all'? Not to be rude, but what are you denying yourself? In what ways are you seeking to save the lost with the compassion and love of Christ?

"Just the other night I stood outside a church and listened to the people's songs rising to heaven when only minutes earlier nobody would meet my eyes or even talk to me as I stood on the steps. If all of us are created in God's image and some of us bear the name 'Christian,' then why do we treat each other so differently? What about those Jesus called, 'the least of these'? I see people inside big churches who live in beautiful homes, wear nice clothes, drive luxury cars, and take exotic vacations, while they don't even look at people like me, at the poor people outside the churches who live in ghettos and trailer parks, travel from state to state looking for jobs, and can't even afford medicine or a home for their kids. With such a bleak future, it's no wonder so many people turn to drugs and alcohol, anything to numb their misery and . . . pain . . . and hopelessness."

As the strength it took to make that speech failed, the hundreds of faces swirled before the vagrant in a disorienting kaleidoscope of melting color. His eyes looked vacant, losing power to focus, as if in a hypnotic trance. He staggered, and an astonished gasp came up from the crowd. He lurched forward, falling toward the first row. The *fwump* of his head slamming against the front pew's hardwood handrest reverberated through the sanctuary, turning stomachs and evoking screams. A warm crimson pool flowed onto the carpet.

Max screamed for a doctor, and in a split second, several cellphones were whipped out of jacket pockets to call

911. A few doctors in the congregation rushed to the man on the floor. Rikki Winslow ran down the altar steps as Max dismissed the congregation and asked them to exit the sanctuary. Rikki zipped off her choir robe and gathered it in a ball. Kneeling down, she held it against the two-inch gash on the man's head. Soon the garment was soaked in blood.

2

On Wednesday morning, the gunmetal skies sent a soft, gray drizzle to the granite headstones and slickened grave markers as a small crowd of darkly dressed figures huddled under umbrellas around a freshly dug grave. At one end stood Max Henry, reading from Psalm 23 to the huddled group of ashen faces. For the first time in his life, Max didn't know quite what to say. For the past few days, he felt as if his inner moorings had been ripped away. He struggled to convey God's comfort for those present at the funeral of the stranger named Jack Manning.

No one in this somber circle of grief had known Jack Manning before last Sunday when he suddenly burst in First Church with a plea for help and a chillingly eerie message that echoed the prophets of old. Some weren't quite sure why they were at this simple graveside service, but they couldn't resist what was drawing them there. Others felt it was simply proper, that it was the right thing to do.

After collapsing near the front row, Jack Manning had been transported to Pasadena General Hospital where he was diagnosed with a severe head injury and a chronic case of influenza. This year's flu epidemic had already hit hospitals so hard that officials asked certain hospitals in Southern California to implement disaster plans, hurrying up some patient discharges in order to make room for others. The flu had already claimed forty-three lives.

Jack was put in the Intensive Care Unit, where his condition worsened through the night. At Jack's bedside, through his intermittent moments of consciousness, Max and Kate learned of the whereabouts of Jack's only child, five-year-old Ashley, who was living with Jack's brother in Las Cruces, New Mexico. Max contacted the brother and made arrangements to bring him with Ashley to California.

Max and Kate paid for the airline tickets and picked the two up at LAX on Monday morning.

After the closing prayer, Max closed his small leather Bible. He looked across the grave to see Kate kneeling down to wipe away the tears running down the cheeks of the little blond-haired Ashley, who clutched a small bunch of white daisies for her daddy.

Knowing he played a small part in this poor child's now orphan state, hot torrents of emotion unleashed a furious downpour of sadness, remorse, and shame on Max. He inhaled for air and unsuccessfully tried to swallow a bitter lump in his throat. Max looked at the deep hole in the ground and heard a message unlike any other he had received in the pastorate. From the wet mud of the sodden grave came a chilling spat of rebuke to the senior pastor of First Church.

You snake! Hypocrite! You shut the kingdom of heaven in men's faces. Greed and self-indulgence know you well.

Max blinked, and his conscience stung from what seemed to be the white-hot tip of a branding iron. He looked up and saw the gathering dispersing itself with quiet good-byes and best wishes. Kate headed toward the car with

Ashley and Jack's brother. Max caught up to her and said he'd be home shortly for lunch.

When all were gone, Max returned to the grave and knelt down next to the casket of Jack Manning. Clutching the bunch of daisies that were left on top of the casket, Max lost himself in a heaving shudder of uncontrollable sobbing. Churning waves of conflicting emotions washed over him as he cried out to God. In the distant clouds above, thunder pealed, and it began to pour.

By Friday, Max still could not shake his experience at Manning's grave site. He spent hours brooding in his upstairs study.

Like fireflies seized by an unseen force, fiery sparks snapped and reeled upward as Max placed another log in the fireplace. He sank back in the leather couch and stared at the glowing fire with a blank, drawn face. The twisting, licking, orangish-yellow flames led his eyes back and forth in a hypnotic dance. The pulsating red coals, tinted by specks of black and surrounded by small clumps of gray ashes, breathed drafts of warm air across the unlit room while ghostly shadows flickered across the knotty pine walls.

Kate had gone to bed some time before, and, like the previous two nights since the funeral of Jack Manning, Max couldn't sleep. He couldn't get the images and events of the past week out of his mind. The front door. Blood. *Quick-Print*. Screams in the sanctuary. Songs of surrender. Ashley. The hospital. White daisies. Ten dollars. Pouring rain. Whispers from the grave.

Lost in a labyrinth of depression, Max felt himself cracking like a broken windshield. *Am I losing my mind?* he wondered. At different times during the day he would burst into tears, excusing himself to go to another room where he could be alone with his grief and pain.

He remembered being in Jack's hospital room late Monday night, moments before he died: Jack lay motionless on his bed, red buzzing lights and piercing alarms sounding from the monitors next to his bed. Doctors and nurses rushed in and cleared the room. Max took a position outside the door and peered in to see the doctor's fist pound on Jack's chest. A cry of *"Clear!"* came from another doctor with defibrillator paddles in both hands. The surging jolt scooped Jack off the bed and flopped him back down like a sack of cement. Two more times the doctors tried to revive him, but by the third, Max knew it was useless.

Now, Max felt like his brain was shattering into a million different pieces. Even Kate mentioned that she'd never seen him this upset, especially for a stranger he barely knew. This depression, grief, remorse, guilt . . . Max wasn't even quite sure what to call it. Why couldn't he have done something different when Jack appeared at the front door? Over and over his mind projected "what if" scenarios on the theater-size screen of his heart. He dragged through each day, limping like a wounded rodent hit by a car, crawling toward the curb. Something was dying inside him. He sensed it. Knew it. Max just wasn't quite sure what it was.

"Hey, Candice, you going to the party tonight at Alpha Chi?" a voice shouted above the splashing sound of a steaming shower in the sorority house bathroom at UCLA.

"If it's anything like the rager at Moose Muldoon's last week, I don't think so!" Candice Sterling shouted back from her stance at the mirror where she stood brushing her long, blond hair.

"You?" the voice yelled back. "Turn down a party?"

The sound of splashing water stopped, and a minute later her roommate, Allison Cordoba, emerged from the shower in a terry cloth robe, her hair done up in a towel.

"I can't believe that. Miss Party Animal herself not showing up at Alpha Chi. Have you seen how many cute guys are in that fraternity? What are you thinking?"

Dressed in black Levi's and a white sweater, Candice set her brush on the counter and turned to Allison. "To be honest, I'm actually getting tired of the whole scene. I've been doing a lot of thinking lately. It's my senior year in college. I just broke it off with Jeff, and I've got to start preparing for on-campus job interviews this spring. I'm ready to have a little more purpose in my life than clawing off drunk underclassmen trying to maul me at frat parties on the weekends."

Allison laughed. "Ooh, that's deep, and you're not even a philosophy major. Sounds like the real issue here is Jeff."

"Well, yeah, it does have a lot to do with Jeff, but it's all connected. We dated for two solid years. During the holidays, we visited each other's families, and I thought his might be my future in-laws. We went to Hawaii together last summer. I honestly thought he was the guy."

"Yeah, the big jerk," Allison chimed in. "He really blew it. Not too many guys get a catch like you. I wonder if he's still seeing that girl."

"Who cares? Not all the roses and notes and apologies in the world could get us back together. I'm just glad he showed his true colors before I agreed to become Mrs. Jeff Thompson." Candice paused and added pensively, "Can you believe we actually talked about getting engaged two weeks before I heard the message she left on his answering machine?"

Allison dried her hair with the towel and responded, "Amazing. That's what I call *good* timing for you and *bad* timing for him. Where are you going tonight anyway?"

"Oh, I'm headed to a campus fellowship meeting Marcy invited me to. There's some speaker she wants me to hear. I thought it sounded interesting."

"You mean those Bible studies she's always going to? You aren't getting religious on me, are you?"

"Religious, no. But for once, I want to do something different on a Friday night. Besides, you've known my family's always attended church in Pasadena. That reminds me . . ." Candice stopped. "I told my folks I'd be home later this weekend."

"Yeah, but just going to church on Sunday is different. For your family, being the blue-blooded pride of Pasadena that they are," Allison piped in a stuffy, English butler voice, "attending church is one of the long list of aristocratic social expectations, along with attending the Charity League functions, the Debutante Ball . . ."

"Enough! I'll debutante you!" Candice countered, dropping her brush. "Take that!"

Candice leapt at Allison and pinned her against the shower door. She dug her knuckles into Allison's scalp in classic *noogie* style—a torture treatment she received as a teenager from her older brothers—while Allison screamed for mercy, which did not come until she offered a complete retraction of her slanderous comments against Candice's good family name. Finally, both girls collapsed on the floor laughing, holding their sides, and vowing future revenge.

Wiping her forehead, Allison looked her best friend in the eyes and said, "Have a fun and sober night tonight. Just don't come back a Jesus freak, okay?"

Very late on Saturday night, Scott Matthews unwrapped a piece of mint gum, slipped it into his mouth, eased open the back door, and gingerly stepped into the kitchen. It was two hours past his curfew. Scott, a junior at Pasadena High School, hoped the gum would mask the smell of beer on his breath. How could his parents ever find out, he wondered, and concluded that they'd never find out. He and his friends had put a few away, and Scott was feeling loose—not drunk but loose enough to feel a good buzz.

He slowly made his way through the darkened house, past the shadowy forms of the living room furniture, rising up the stairs into the formless, black void above him. Feeling his way up the cool, smooth banister, Scott stepped gently, carefully, holding out one hand as a guide until he touched the knob of the door at the top of the stairs.

When Scott walked through the doorway, he shut the door behind him, let go of the knob, stepped right and moved two paces forward; he felt his left foot catch on something. His body twisted as his foot was propelled backward by a sliding, unseen force. A light, floating sensation filled his body.

Wham! Scott's face slammed against the hardwood floor. The force of the fall expelled air from his lungs with a heavy whack. The right side of his face stung as if he'd received a powerful, wet slap. Scott lay on the floor, motionless. He tried to catch his breath, doing anything possible to get air into his oxygen-depleted lungs. He braced himself for the worst, his heart pounding.

Man! he thought. *This is it . . . I'm nailed.*

He waited for his folks' bedroom door to swing open. All he heard was silence. Scott didn't move. He didn't dare. His head pounded, and he began to taste a bitter, salty fluid in his mouth. He moved his tongue around to feel where it was coming from—lower lip, right side. He wiggled his tongue and touched the fleshy, blood-draining hole. Scott winced in pain.

Hearing nothing from down the hallway, Scott finally rolled over and looked down at his feet. A glowing, greenish skull and crossbones with menacing eyes stared at him—Kelly's skateboard. Her stupid, glow-in-the-dark skateboard.

She's dead, Scott murmured under his breath. *How many times has she been told to keep that lame thing in the garage?*

Scott picked himself up and staggered toward his room. The red numbers on his clock radio glowed 2:06 A.M. Flipping the closet light on, Scott went to his mirror and pulled his lip down. His upper teeth made a perfect match with the two jagged divots in his lower lip.

After I dismantle that board, he schemed, *I'm going to dismantle her face.* Seventh-grade sisters, what a pain.

Scott walked back into the hallway and headed toward his parents' room. He turned the carved, brass doorknob and poked his head through the door. Two supine figures lay motionless in rumpled blankets, the sound of heavy breathing hovering over the bed.

"Dad," Scott whispered as quietly as possible. "Daaad . . . I'm home."

The figure on the right side of the bed stirred, and a groaning head lifted slightly above the pillow. "What time is it?" David Matthews moaned.

"Just before twelve."

"That's three weeks in a row, Scott. Good job."

"Yeah, well, I'm trying," Scott lied. "Just like we talked about."

"See ya in the morning. Night, Scott."

"Night, Dad."

Scott pulled the door closed, rolled his eyes, and walked back to his room. *Whew! That was close.*

After Jack's dramatic speech at church and subsequent death, the gossip around First Church was as absurd, extreme, and colorful as the mountains of trash left on Colorado Boulevard after the Rose Parade. Nearly everyone had an opinion about the incident. Some blamed the ushers for not whisking Jack away. They thought the accident never would have happened if Pastor Henry had intervened sooner. Some saw Jack as crazy and thought that mentally ill people should not be allowed to walk the streets near churches or playgrounds. Others figured that the stranger probably concocted the story about his dead wife and homeless little girl in order to get money—you read about schemes like that in the paper all the time. They thought the Benevolence Fund should be reserved only for church members who are recently divorced or widowed. There was even talk of hiring a security company to patrol the parking lot and front steps on Sunday mornings and at evening events during the week. Many First Church members simply refused to participate in the flurry of gossip and speculation. "My goodness," one exclaimed at a midweek church meeting, "a man just died; have some compassion!"

The Sunday morning following the funeral was as clear and beautiful as the week before. The snow-covered peaks of Mt. Baldy and the surrounding mountains could be seen in the distance as the members and families of First Church streamed into the service. After two short hymns, Max rose to the pulpit in a slow and sullen gait. Wearing a grim expression, he appeared to be in pain. He gripped the pulpit with both hands and slowly panned his eyes across the congregation. It was one of the largest crowds he'd seen at First Church.

Max opened his Bible, and the image of a falling, bleeding Jack Manning stirred in his mind. Max had spent absolutely no time in sermon prep the past week, so there were no notes to arrange in front of him. The regular attendees who were familiar with his pulpit habits and mannerisms noticed this and silently questioned if this service would also be full of surprises.

The beginning of Max's sermon was flat and unremarkable—a rare strikeout. He stood stiffly at the lectern, never once leaving it to walk near the front pews and down the center aisle. His hands made limp, weak gestures that only matched the monotone quality of his voice. His speech was filled with stammers and long pauses. He seemed to be groping for the right words. The events of the past week had obviously shaken him. Some members wondered whether the Manning family had threatened to sue the church.

After ten minutes of this, Max closed his Bible and stepped away from the pulpit. He walked down the altar steps, his gaze meeting the startled faces on the First Church members seated before him. Max choked back tears as he continued.

"This past week I conducted the funeral for Jack Manning, the man who interrupted the service last week. As most of you can imagine, the past week has been difficult for Kate and me, particularly when Jack's daughter, Ashley, and his brother stayed with us on Monday, Tuesday, and Wednesday nights. I am devastated over what happened. I've never experienced grief like I have the past few days. This stranger's outburst and what he had to say last Sunday in church has made a powerful and lasting impression on me. I'd be lying to you, myself, and even God, if I tried to hide my reaction to what he said and the manner in which he died. His life and death have compelled me to ask the question as I never asked before, 'What *does* it mean to follow Jesus?'"

He stopped a moment, wrestling with what to say next. "Jack Manning's words last Sunday were a direct challenge to Christianity as it is practiced in our church and in churches all across America. I have spent many sleepless nights this week reflecting on his words. I am determined to have his questions answered in my own life. Last week, I spoke about what it means to follow Christ according to 1 Peter 2:21. As Jack noted, I didn't clearly explain what I meant when I spoke of following Christ. And I can't think of a more appropriate time than right now to propose to you a specific plan that has been forming in my mind the past few days."

Max stopped again and looked into the faces of his people. At any other time, Max might have felt more than a little intimidated by the challenge he was about to put forth to the wealthy and powerful of his congregation. He had witnessed more than a few friends in ministry weakened in their spiritual resolve by the power of affluence.

Max had experienced that uneasiness a few times before, but right now, he didn't care. He wasn't interested in pleasing others. His grief had exposed him, revealing a heart filled with self-absorption and ego-driven pride. He was pulling away from the docks of self-interest and comfort, and if he was the only one in the boat, so be it. As he looked around, Max saw something that gave him hope. He saw caring and earnest faces on many of the men and women of First Church. The looks on their faces reflected a sincere desire to love God not by mere words. In the fourth row, he saw Paul Wickman, the mutual fund manager of the most-talked-about company on Wall Street. At thirty-two years old, he was bright, intelligent, married to a beautiful wife, and raising two kids. Max respected Paul for the way he moved among financial titans with humility and sincerity.

There was Victorio Gennaro, a third-generation Italian with a hearty laugh and a big heart. He was "Vic" to anyone he met once and a longtime member of First Church. Years ago, Vic's grandparents had come over from Italy and opened a small leather shop in downtown Los Angeles. Vic worked the business with his dad as a boy and, eventually, grew Gennaro Leatherworks into a nationwide chain known for high-quality, expensive leather goods. Behind Vic and his wife sat David and Jessica Matthews, one of First Church's many young professional couples. He sold life insurance, and she was a third-grade teacher at Longfellow Elementary, which was just down the street from the Henrys' home.

Across the aisle, there was the unpretentious Sam Baker, a no-nonsense trucker who drove an old Dodge pickup. Sam was a bit of a standout among the First Church members, albeit a very wealthy one. His company, USA Trucking, well known for their hokey, late-night television commercials, was one of the largest residential trucking companies in the nation. Candice Sterling, a stunning UCLA student who majored in marketing and was active in her sorority, sat with her parents, longtime members of First Church.

Sitting in the back, where all the high school students usually congregated, was seventeen-year-old Alex Powers, a computer phenom who helped major corporations develop their Internet infrastructure. Alex was so gifted at math and programming languages that he was allowed to take a number of courses at the California Institute of Technology. Down the row next to some girlfriends sat Rikki Winslow, whose voice and youthful radiance were well known to everyone at First Church. Nearby was Gina Page, a soft-spoken young woman who, along with her brother Brock, had inherited millions as children when their parents were killed when their family's private jet crashed in the mountains of Colorado. Miraculously, Gina and Brock survived, but not without vivid memories of the crash and the pain of growing up without a father and mother. At twenty-one, Gina still lived at her family's mansion estate in nearby San Marino with Florence, her aunt.

As he looked into those faces, Max grew in boldness over what he was about to present, but that boldness was tempered by the acute awareness that he had no idea where this thing was going to land. Max took a deep breath and said, "Let me be blunt. What I'm going to propose may initially seem strange or unusual or impossible, although I think it could be one of the most exciting tasks we could undertake. My challenge to you is this: I want you to make an honest promise for one year not to do anything without first asking yourselves, 'What would Jesus do?'"

There was no audible response in the audience as the stunned congregation kept every eye glued on Max.

"Once you have asked yourself that question, each of you will follow Jesus exactly as you know how, regardless of the consequences. This is a promise I have decided to keep for myself, whether I stand alone or with a company of volunteers. I have also discussed this fully with Kate. Both my and Kate's future conduct will be based upon this question, with the Scriptures and the Holy Spirit as our guide, so it should be fully understood by all First Church members that any decision we are involved with regarding this church will also be affected by this new standard. At the close of this service, I would like every person who is interested in making this promise to meet afterward in the fellowship hall so we can talk about the details of the plan.

"The challenge seems simple on the face of it, but I expect it to change my life and yours: Those who wish to accept this challenge and to follow in Jesus' footsteps as best as they know how will ask themselves 'What would Jesus do?' in any and all situations from this day forward."

3

After the service, Max walked into the First Church fellowship hall expecting to see perhaps a handful of parishioners wary about participating in the 'What would Jesus do?' promise. To his surprise, the large room with a small kitchen, Formica tables, cushioned folding chairs, comfortable couches, and a fireplace in the far corner was filled with over fifty people.

Earlier, when he concluded the service with a final prayer, there had certainly been a buzz among the members, not unlike the previous Sunday. As people greeted one another afterward, the looks on everyone's faces made it obvious what they were thinking about. The members were a bit astonished, some taken back, by this new-to-them definition of Christian discipleship. What Max had proposed was certainly honorable, they thought, but there were considerable differences of opinion on what it meant to follow in Jesus' footsteps.

Outside in the front courtyard, dozens of animated conversations took place regarding Max's challenge. Small groups of women huddled to talk about how awful Max looked and how terrible his sermon was. Another group of women admired his honesty and willingness to take a risk. A few professors from the local seminary and colleges debated the differences between the literal and mythical interpretation of discipleship found in Scripture. Under a tree on the lawn, the high school and college students talked about Max's courage and said how cool it was for him to stand up for Jack Manning. Some businessmen, one of them a church elder, questioned the potential financial impact of Max's new plan on the church. Gradually, a number of people made their way to the fellowship hall, while the majority of the congregation slinked away to their cars after making concerted attempts to let the others know they had prior brunch commitments at the club or what kind of monsters their kids turned into without a nap.

Max gave a weak smile as he looked at the many faces, young and old, before him in the fellowship hall. Alex Powers, David and Jessica Matthews, Paul Wickman, Candice Sterling, Vic Gennaro, Gina Page, and Sam Baker stood out for him among the people gathered to hear about the next steps proposed by their pastor.

Max shut the door and stood before the group, again searching for words. His face was pale, and his hands trembled. As he had done for the past several days, Max reflected on the thoughts, words, attitudes, and motivations that had defined his character for as long as he'd been in the ministry. He thought about everything he had ever learned and taught about Christian discipleship. Everything he knew was wrong, or at least the way he went about his own life. Before him stood his people, God's people, wondering what the next steps were, and the thought of leading them now almost made Max sick to his stomach. As a pastor, he had bought a lie, packaged it, and sold it as God's truth. He had preached the safe, broad road, but now he felt himself standing at an old, wooden gate leading to the narrow way. He had led the First Church congregation for nine years, but now all he sensed was brokenness and a deep inadequacy of what it meant to follow Jesus.

In a quiet voice, Max asked everyone in the room to pray with him. "Lord, we are here to begin an adventure with you. We come very uncertain about the future, but with total trust that you will guide and direct us step by step."

With the first words of the prayer, each person in the room, some standing, others in chairs, even a few kneeling, sensed a strange and wonderful presence within their hearts. The presence of the Spirit moved upon them with the warmth of a soft blanket. They all felt it. Drops of tears fell to folded hands below. As Max continued to pray out loud, many prayed quietly in their hearts, offering the promise of a yielded self and asking for strength to follow in a humble and authentic new way. An invigorating wave of freedom washed over every heart as if the room had been flooded by a rushing river of pure, clear water.

For several moments after the prayer closed, the room was filled with silence and a strange sense of awe. Pastor Max's cheeks streamed with tears, spent from the relentless pressure of the past few days. Some sobbed like little children, their heads buried in their arms, as if they had been released from a dark, inner closet of guilt and shame. Never before had this group experienced the profound, intimate embrace of the Spirit.

Max began to speak quietly. "Before asking any of you to take this one-year promise, I want you to know that this is a promise I am making myself. I can't expect any of you to be or do anything I am not willing to do first. I want us all to understand that we are promising to do everything in our lives by first asking the question, 'What would Jesus do?' regardless of what the consequences may be. This has been the most powerful week of my life, and the events of the past week have initiated an intense, personal transformation in me. I have discovered a deep dissatisfaction with my previous understanding of what it meant to follow Christ. I'm also suffering with a broken heart, and I need to deal with my grief in the coming months. But I'm compelled to live out this new promise. I know it's not something I can do on my own. Never before have I felt led by God's love in such a clear and distinct way, and it's obvious that many of you sense the same tug. Do we all understand what we are promising to do here?"

From near the fireplace, Rikki Winslow raised her hand and said with a tinge of hesitation, "I have a question. Asking what Jesus would do could be very confusing, especially when it depends on who's asking the question. Who's to say what is the right thing to do when there are so many options to choose from? We live in a society where people think that 'right' is whatever you want to make it. I mean, there's a big difference between now and the time when Jesus walked the earth. How I am supposed to know what he would do?"

"That's a good question. I certainly don't have all the answers I used to," Max replied. "But, the one thing we can depend on, that we can really trust, is the Holy Spirit. I've been asking myself those same questions lately, and what I've found most helpful are the words of Christ to his disciples in John 16, verse 13: 'But when he, the Spirit of truth, comes, he will guide you into all truth. He will not speak on his own; he will speak only what he hears, and he will tell you what is yet to come.' This promise of Jesus to provide the guidance of the Spirit will help each one of us determine what Jesus would do in the different situations we will encounter."

After clearing his voice, Paul Wickman spoke. "What are we supposed to say when others challenge us by saying Jesus would have acted in a different way?"

A number of heads nodded in agreement and looked at Max. "That is something you won't be able to avoid. I can't say you won't encounter any conflict. You have to be honest with God and honest with yourself. God promises to guide and direct you, but that doesn't mean following Christ will be easy."

Candice Sterling spoke next. She told everyone in the room that the previous night was the first time she had let God into her heart. She had gone to a campus Bible study with a friend and was captivated by the words of the speaker. She'd always thought of herself as a Christian because her family went to church. But after she listened to what the speaker had to say about following Christ and then compared that to her own lifestyle, she knew she had to make some changes. All of this was so new to her, she hoped the others in the room would help her out.

Max thanked Candice for her words and then fielded a number of other questions before concluding, "When people are loved and not judged, shown compassion and not shunned, there won't be much of an argument. Christ's message of love and forgiveness wasn't complicated. Some of it will be common sense and simply treating people the way we would like to be treated. Other aspects will be more difficult. We need to stop being so selfish with our time and money and resources. I can't imagine Jesus giving us his example without also providing us the strength and insight to follow that example. Most of us know what we need to do in our heads, but we need to put our hearts into action by acting upon what we know . . . regardless of the results. That's the only way this promise will work. Agreed?"

Heads nodded throughout the room as Max thought about the nature of this group of believers. They weren't about to form a new committee or create a new program with a jazzy-sounding name to entice people to sign up. How many great movements of the Spirit eventually became like political campaigns, Christians just jumping on the proverbial bandwagon in search of a new spin on God? It reminded Max of the "27th Annual End Times Conference" he read about in the *Los Angeles Times* every year. "Mountaintop experiences" and the good feelings that followed were only as good as the change seen in one's character and lifestyle; the only real measure of change was sincere love and action. No amount of emotion can permanently change a stubborn will. Max vowed to keep this promise simple and sincere. This promise—and this group—was not about words but action.

After Max closed in a final prayer, the group agreed to meet weekly after each service. In this meeting they would discuss what happened during the week as they followed Jesus in their schools, professions, friendships, homes, and neighborhoods. Several people mentioned that this would be a good way to learn from one another and provide the support needed to keep such a promise.

As they left the fellowship hall, Max greeted and hugged each person. There was a vibrant spirit of enthusiasm over the newfound community they'd just experienced and the adventure the group had just embarked upon. Afterward, Max headed back to the sanctuary. There, near the front row where Jack Manning fell, he knelt and prayed for nearly an hour.

Max sensed a profound change in his life. He was thankful that the confusion and depression of the past few days were lifting, and he didn't even think about what could happen in the city of Pasadena as a result of this action by those fifty people. In a land known for devastating earthquakes and wild brushfires, a small spark ignited First Church like a candle waiting to be burned. Little did anyone fully realize what God could do with one spark.

On Monday afternoon, from the fifty-seventh floor of the Daewoo building in the heart of L.A.'s financial district, Paul Wickman stood by the window of his large office and looked out toward Santa Monica, the Pacific Ocean glimmering in the distance. What a wild day, Paul reflected, as he marveled at the view from his corner office.

The Dow Jones Index had gone in the tank from the opening bell of the stock market, dropping a hundred points within minutes of the start of the session. The downward spiral was triggered by speculation about a forthcoming interest rate meeting by the Federal Reserve Board. By noon, the market was down an additional eighty points, which ignited a flurry of sell orders by shareholders. Throughout the day, Paul and his cadre of hardworking assistants, analysts, and traders monitored their cash reserves like a nervous teenager combing his hair on a first date, constantly checking their positions on the stocks held in the Millennium Star portfolio. Paul made a few tough decisions to issue sell orders on stocks that had favorable long-term prospects but hadn't performed strongly for the last two quarters. Conservative by nature, Paul maintained the integrity of the fund and its stellar performance by knowing how and when to weight the portfolio's cash position depending on market conditions.

By the end of the session, the market rallied and eventually gave up only thirty points for the day. Paul was tired yet relieved the market recovered. Piled high on his desk were stacks of third-quarter earnings estimates and analyst's reports for the two hundred or so companies that comprised the Millennium Star mutual fund holdings. At thirty-two, Paul was one of the youngest and most talked about mutual fund managers west of Wall Street. A Wharton Business School graduate, Paul rose before dawn every morning and snaked his way downtown through L.A. traffic from his home near the Wrigley Mansion in Pasadena. Twenty minutes before the opening bell rang at the New York Stock Exchange, Paul was always at his large, black lacquer desk, reviewing the day's batting order of which stocks to buy, hold, or sell.

Hundreds of thousands of Americans—schoolteachers, factory workers, widows living on pensions, self-employed business owners, government employees—entrusted their savings, pensions, IRAs, 401(k) and SEP plans to the Millennium Star, which boasted a ten-year annualized return of 19 percent. Larger than the gross national product of some small nations, the Millennium Star Fund portfolio held 8.5 billion dollars in diversified assets from various sectors of the economy: health care, technology, finance, utilities, transportation, energy. As a growth fund, the Millennium Star balanced large, blue-chip stocks with well-known consumer companies favored by millions. Not only was the Millennium Star an attractive fund for thousands of Americans who knew the benefits of saving for the future, but it also had the lowest management fees in the industry.

Paul walked over and flipped off his Bloomberg machine for the day. He picked up a summary sheet for how the Millennium Star fared for the day. Scanning the list of holdings in the fund, Paul shook his head. All day long, in between the rush of sell orders, emergency meetings with analysts, a phone call from his wife, Roberta, reminding him not to go home but to meet her—and not be late this time— at the Pasadena Civic Auditorium for tonight's symphony, constantly monitoring the market, and forgetting to eat lunch, Paul couldn't get yesterday's meeting at the church out of his mind. He had never experienced anything quite like it. Paul couldn't help but feel that accepting Pastor Max's challenge was the first step in what had been a latent conviction in his heart he'd been ignoring for some time. He had been experiencing a growing dissatisfaction with his relationship with God. He felt it had been a waffling commitment at best. Before yesterday, if Paul had measured his faithfulness to the things of God by the same standards he scrutinized Fortune 500 companies, he would have issued a sell order long ago. But now, after making the one-year promise Max proposed, Paul sensed a degree of confidence and freedom he'd never felt before. He did wonder, though, how he was going to talk with Roberta about it.

She hadn't joined him in the fellowship hall after the service. Roberta and he had driven to church separately because they had different plans for the day. She had a lunch date with the kids at her parents' home in La Canada-Flintridge, a neighboring town of old wealth and majestic oaks. He had planned an early afternoon tee time at Annandale Country Club.

After nine holes of slow play, four double bogeys, and only one par, Paul had thanked his partners and called it a day. It was obvious his mind was nowhere near the course and he might have well used, as his partners had remarked, a backhoe to putt.

Paul's poor performance hadn't bothered him. After feeling the Spirit's touch at the meeting that morning, what could compare to those few minutes of intimate fellowship and heartfelt prayer? He hadn't known most of the people in the room, but he'd never seen over a dozen people openly cry in public like that. Except at a funeral.

Millennium's offices were now, for the most part, quiet. After the market closed, most of the younger staff members usually blew off to the bars or health clubs to either drink away their stress or sweat it off. Paul leaned against his desk and stared at the summary sheet. He loosened his tie and slowly tapped one corner of the paper with his index finger. Thinking.

A question gradually surfaced in his mind, its initial presence a bit startling: *If Jesus was the head of this mutual fund, what would he do?*

Paul scanned the various companies and industries represented on the list. Here was a chemical manufacturer that had outstanding earnings but that was also repeatedly at odds with the Environmental Protection Agency for polluting key tributaries that flowed into the Mississippi River. And here was a large defense contractor that made land mines no bigger than a hockey puck but were capable of blowing off a grown man's leg. This contractor was immensely profitable because of large foreign contracts with countries at war in Eastern Europe, Africa, and parts of Asia. He'd seen more than one news report on how orphanages in many of these war-torn countries were filled with small children missing one or both legs after chasing an errant ball into a minefield.

Going down the list, Paul made mental notes as he carefully considered what business each of these companies was really in. Some of them looked innocent enough. Tennis shoes . . . what was immoral about footwear? Except for their outrageous prices and the pressure kids put on their parents to pay those prices, this company had soundly rewarded its shareholders over the years. But there was also the issue of their manufacturing plants overseas where laborers were paid pitiful amounts of money for a day's labor. There were also a number of stocks Millennium held in the entertainment industry—from shock-jock radio stations to daytime television companies that produced sex-laden soap operas and talk shows that enticed millions of viewers with such brazen, mindless topics as "Serial Killers and the Women They Marry."

Previously, Paul evaluated companies based solely on earnings reports, the company's management team, debt ratios, annual growth rate, and the competitiveness of the particular industry, along with other general market factors. Never had he made moral or value judgments about a company and its impact on society as a whole. Neither did Millennium's shareholders, he reasoned, since one mutual fund can contain hundreds of companies. Unless a shareholder investigated each individual stock in Millennium's annual report, they willingly invested in companies whose practices may run opposite to their personal beliefs. Paul wondered what people were supposed to do. How could people invest for their futures without compromising their beliefs? Over a long investment horizon, the stock market offered historically better returns than real estate, precious metals, entrepreneurial ventures, or any other investment vehicle. People couldn't pull out their life's savings and retirement income only to leave it under an old mattress.

He couldn't imagine sitting down with his management team and giving them a whole new investment strategy based on a promise he had made at church. By nature, Paul was calm and not one to make rash decisions, so the idea of immediately dumping stocks seemed a bit extreme. But for the first time in his life, he was willing to begin to pray about his investment decisions in a deeper way than just, "Let me continue to make the most profitable moves." Right now, Paul needed time to think and the wisdom to know when and how to act. The question, "What would Jesus do?" *was* intriguing. Paul thought about giving Pastor Max a call for lunch this week. He certainly couldn't be the only one thinking about the ethical ramifications of such a powerful question. He wondered what kinds of questions and dilemmas were being faced by others who had attended yesterday's meeting after church.

Paul shot a glance at the clock on his desk and saw that it was well after five. "Traffic's going to be terrible," he muttered with a grimace. Roberta would be livid if he was late to the symphony again.

To the west, the sky was giving up its last glimmers of daylight by frosting a long band of high clouds with a rich patina of light green, salmon pink, and soft blue. The white square shapes of office windows in the surrounding skyscrapers appeared in a checkerboard pattern with the charcoal black darkness of offices that had emptied for the day.

Paul loaded into his briefcase some reports to read after the symphony and walked toward the glass door of his office. He clicked off the lights and briskly walked along a long row of cubicles to the elevator doors, not sure if he would make it on time or not.

A few days after Sunday's meeting in the fellowship hall, Max stood in his study next to his computer, nursing a cup of lukewarm coffee. The soft, whirring hum of the laser printer produced a warm, single sheet of paper. He picked it up and reviewed the half page that had taken him over an hour to write. On his desk was a copy of First Church's old mission statement, a document that he and the elders had rewritten over a year ago. In it, they had outlined the vision and values and mission and purpose of First Church, its ministries, programs, and responsibilities to First Church members. Now, as Max thought about the differences between that document and the new one in his hand, it seemed like the old one read like the dull CC & R documents of a homeowners association.

The sheet in his hand, which wasn't really a new mission or vision statement, was as plain as a country girl in a summer dress. Max planned on sharing it with the elders at their next meeting. He didn't want to disrupt the church or force others to make promises against their will, but he wanted to be up front about changes, necessary changes, that were happening inside him. He had earnestly prayed for the Spirit to direct his steps, and this was his first pass at what he hoped was real and lasting change.

In bold print, the title read:

A Few Things Jesus Would Do in This Church

1. Live in a simple, unpretentious manner.

2. Preach against hypocrisy in the church regardless of whom he upset.
3. Serve the rich *and* the poor in practical, concrete ways. Minister to the people of First Church and the surrounding community without regard to race, religion, or economic status.
4. Delay gratification of immediate personal wants. Seek to build the kingdom of God first by concerning himself with the greater needs of humanity.
5. Help families and their children in the greater Pasadena area live drug-free lives.
6. Become a friend to the ministers and the poor of Los Angeles.
7. Forego extravagant expenditures and willingly give the money to a family in need.

As Max read over the seven items that would serve as a practical framework for asking himself what Jesus would do, he let out a slow whistle. This was certainly a lot to live up to. Inside, Max felt these ideas—at least for now—were the right things to do. Still, this list was foreign to his previous behavior. He felt as if God was completely rewiring him from the inside out. It seemed that practically everything he had prepared himself to do as a minister—everything he learned in seminary or from church attendance and evangelism seminars, books, tapes, and church growth newsletters—focused on the mechanics of ministry. It wasn't that those things were wrong, but perhaps he was wrong in focusing only on those tasks. He had missed the spirit of Christ, the heart and depth of God's Spirit, the law of love.

The list before him was so, what could he call it, so simple. It wasn't a formula. It didn't guarantee results or greater church attendance. If there was a narrow road, short of his holing up in a monastery somewhere in the African desert, this was certainly it. In actuality, Max was sure this list lacked the depth and power of what Jesus would really do if he were in his place, but it was a start. If this promise, this vow before God, was going to be anything of substance to him or anyone else, Max knew he at least had to outline a few concrete ways to follow the steps of Jesus that would require some personal sacrifice on his part. This list wasn't about earning God's favor or working his way into heaven, but Max knew that by giving himself away, he would ultimately discover the deeper purposes of knowing and loving God.

As Max sat back down at his desk, the words of Matthew 10:39, which he had memorized years ago, resonated deep within him: "Whoever finds his life will lose it, and whoever loses his life for my sake will find it." Though Max had been in ministry all his life, he could now see that, behind much of his work in the church, was the desire to enhance his image, his ego, and his prominence in the community. Until Jack Manning came into his life, Max never realized how tired he was of building his own kingdom. God, in his grace, had allowed First Church to prosper and grow despite Max's own blindness and failings.

Looking at the list again, Max felt ready to relearn everything he knew about leadership and loving others. Ever since Sunday's meeting, he couldn't stop talking with Kate about the changes he felt going on inside himself. He was ready to stop being the "professional" minister, ready to stop allowing his moods to be dictated by the weather, the attendance, what people thought of his sermon, the assumptions he placed on volunteers' time, or what an asset First Church was to the community and the arts. It wasn't until that cold rainy day at Forest Lawn Cemetery that Max discovered how full of himself he really was. Never before saw himself as selfish. Or greedy. Or egotistical.

For the first time since he entered ministry and was begging, pleading with God to give him an associate pastor position somewhere, anywhere, Max was ready to get out of God's way and learn to follow. He wanted to serve, to be involved with something about others and not himself.

Lost in his thoughts, Max barely heard the phone ring. Picking it up, he heard the voice of Vic Gennaro on the line.

"Max, this is Vic. Hey, I was thinking about what we talked about after church the other morning. I was speaking to one of my employees who attends the Spanish-speaking church down in South Pas, and we've got an idea. You know the pastor there, don't you?"

"Yes, Emilio Alvarez. I've known him for some time."

"Well, give him a call. I want the two of you to come to my factory on Friday morning to speak with some of the workers in the factory. They have a lunch Bible study every Friday, and they want to hear about what happened at First Church last week."

"How many people we talking about, Vic?"

"Oh, not many," Vic replied in a nonchalant voice. "About a hundred or so."

"You've got to be kidding!"

"I'm not, Pastor. When you threw out that challenge on Sunday, I went after it like a grizzly bear swatting salmon. I've been coming up with a few ideas about how to make things better for the people here at work. You just do your part and get here on Friday, comprende, partner?"

"Yeah, I got it," Max promised. "Hey, Vic?"

"What is it?"

"Last Sunday was pretty amazing, wasn't it?"

"Yeah. It was," Vic replied. "I think we're in for a wild ride though."

"Hang onto your hat, then. I wouldn't have it any other way. I'll see you Friday."

4

rande double skim mocha, dressed," the cash register attendant yelled. She collected a small wad of one-dollar bills from a woman dressed in sweats who had a serious case of bedhead, tousled hair and the Thursday morning paper in hand.

Standing at a hissing espresso machine at the Starbucks coffeehouse on Lake Street, silver pitcher and thermometer in hand, Don Marsh mimicked in a low, sarcastic voice, "Grande double skim mocha. Latte this, latte that." He looked around the halogen-lit room filled with sleek black chairs, brown maple counters, coffee cups of all shapes and sizes, music CD's, bright coffee bean posters on the walls, and bold, colorful signs announcing the latest exotic blend. *Same place, same thing,* Don thought to himself, wondering how long he would last at this job.

He poured the mocha into a paper cup wrapped with a piece of corrugated cardboard, set it on the counter in front of the caffeine achiever who ordered it, offered a plastic smile, and said, "Thanks for coming to Starbucks. Have a *great* day!"

Just then, the bell on the front door jingled. In walked Gina Page, a welcome sight so early. Not hard on the eyes either.

"Hi, Don, how ya doing?"

"Doing okay, Gina. Whattaya got there?" Don asked, pointing to the stack of books and pads of paper under her arm.

"Oh, some sketches I need to finish for my interior design class. They're due tomorrow, and I'm *so* far behind."

Don shook his headful of curls, a strange grin surfacing on his face. "I don't understand you, Gina. You don't need to take any design classes. What are you even doing in the Design Center to begin with? If I were you, I'd be traveling Europe right now, hiking the Swiss Alps, paddling the canals of Venice, getting chased by bulls in Spain. Or I'd be on my yacht in Micronesia hopping from island to island, cracking coconuts open for lunch. But no, here it is, seven-thirty on Thursday morning, and you're doing work for a class to get a career you don't even need. You could buy that school in cash if you wanted! I do not get it."

Gina rolled her eyes, her irises the color of the dark espresso Don was pouring into a white cup. "Yeah, right, Don. And what are you doing up so early this morning?"

Don laughed in an incredulous, high-pitched voice, "Unlike you, I *have* to work!"

"No, you don't. It's a choice."

"*Choice?* Gimme a break. I could also *choose* not to pay for my classes, and *choose* to get kicked out of my apartment, and *choose* to live on the street like a homeless person."

"Well, I've chosen to do something creative with my life. I want to have more purpose than sitting around and watching soaps and Oprah all week long. In fact, last Sunday at church, the pastor got up and asked everyone to . . ."

"Whoa, now wait a minute. That's turning a corner. You don't need to give me any of that God stuff. I've watched enough TV church channels to know I don't want religion. I mean, have you seen that guy with the pompadour toupee and his makeup-plastered wife who beg old people for money?"

"Oh, come on, Don! Not every church is like what you see on television. That's like thinking every TV show you watch is real."

"Yeah, but other TV shows don't ask for money either. If I spend my money in response to an infomercial, at least I get a blender or some new and improved car wax sent to me. Those spiritual infomercials ask for your money but give you nothing in return."

"Well, maybe those old people get something good out of it. You still can't judge every church based on what you see on TV. There are a lot of good things happening in churches, and like I was saying before, you should see what happened at my church."

"You go to First Church, right? That's a perfect example of a lot of money in one place that's not doing anybody else any good. Some of those people come in here after church on Sunday, and they're pushy, demanding, and lousy tippers."

"Oh, Don," Gina said in an exasperated voice. "You're such a pessimist."

"Me? I'm not a pessimist. I'm a realist who sees things for what they are."

Gina narrowed her eyes and said in a quiet voice, "Money's good for some things, Don, but not everything. I know plenty of very wealthy people in this city, even at First Church, who're miserable with all their riches and their status and their toys. It doesn't matter if someone has a lot or a little; people are looking for something more in their lives." Gina stared Don in the eyes. "And it doesn't come from money."

Don stared back, unconvinced. "I wish I had your problem. You should tell that to your brother. That guy's got a lifestyle I would die for. Is he still in the Sierras?"

"Yes, he's off climbing another mountain somewhere . . . or snowboarding, I think." Gina paused, trying to change the tone of the conversation. "Brock likes to play, but does he ever seem happy to you? He's a perfect example of someone looking for purpose in his life. He's always on the search for the next big adventure, the next big thrill."

"I know I could be very happy having unlimited means to travel anywhere in the world," Don replied. "Let me tell you how thrilling it is to make a zillion killer mochas every day."

"Speaking of coffee, do I get a discount because I know you?"

"No way, Miss Moneybags. Your kind pays full price."

"Can we call a truce on our religious war?"

"Hey, I didn't bring it up."

"Truce, Don?"

"Truce."

Don and Gina laughed as he poured her a fresh cup of house blend.

"Here, it's on the house."

"Good. In lieu of payment I'll take you to First Church some Sunday."

"Yeah, right. I think my Sundays are booked for this life and the next." Don chuckled as Gina smiled and made her way to one of the small black tables.

When Gina sat down, she glanced down at the front page of the *Pasadena Star-News*, which someone had left on the table. A short article in the lower right-hand corner immediately caught her attention:

MacArthur Park Soup Kitchen Closes

The MacArthur Park Soup Kitchen was forced to close its doors to the needy and homeless yesterday due to mismanagement, lack of funding, and violations of health and safety codes. Serving an average of four thousand meals a week, the kitchen was responsible for helping needy individuals and families throughout the area.

After repeated attempts to secure government funding for its programs and the ouster of the center's controversial director, Peter Hampton, the kitchen was forced to shut down. Glen Davies, a member of the soup kitchen board, said the center will be immediately put up for sale to pay outstanding debts. When asked about the kitchen's closure, Paul Dempster, a local homeless man, said, "I don't know what I'm going to do for food . . . this place is all I've got."

Gina put the newspaper down and took a sip of her coffee.

What if, she wondered. *What if?*

She suddenly gathered up her books, placed a lid on her coffee, waved good-bye to Don, and rushed out the door.

West of Highway 395, high above the sheep town of Bishop that nestles along the eastern slopes of the Sierra Nevada range, rests the Palisades Glacier. From the towering fourteen-thousand-foot peaks above the vast snowfield, Brock Page's winter tent appeared as a tiny yellow M&M among the white glacial sea and rocky moraine. Far in the distance to the south, a mixture of tan and rust-colored dust clouds danced across the dry Owens River lake bed. Stirred by a cold winter wind, their opaque, transmuted forms blew south toward Southern California.

Standing at the precipice of a steep powder bowl, the twenty-two-year-old mountaineer clicked into his snowboard bindings, yanked the straps on his twenty-pound daypack tight, and grabbed his aluminum ice ax.

"Ready to go, Jay?"

"Not yet, Mr. Page." His buddy exhaled and took another swig of water from a water bottle. "We just hit the summit, and you can't sit still for a minute. Relax and enjoy the view."

Brock stuffed the tail end of a candy bar in his mouth and barked with a brown, syrupy goo on his teeth, "C'mon! The snow's getting soft. You're the one who couldn't get out of your sleeping bag this morning. I'm not going to dig your rear out if an avalanche falls on your head!"

"Avalanche, smavalanche," Jay snapped back as he threw his pack over his shoulder and walked toward his snowboard. "You saw the snow layers yourself. The snow-pack is as firm as the Hoover Dam."

Though Brock and Jay constantly sparred with verbal jabs, each took backcountry safety seriously. Neither would think of heading down a steep powder bowl without first digging a pit to examine the snow crystals for warning clues of avalanche danger.

Jay was right. The snow conditions were good, but Brock always prided himself on self-reliance and his ability to take calculated risks. What he didn't like was taking stupid risks, like snowboarding down a mountainside too late in the day. He always felt better getting up and down a peak quickly, before the late afternoon sun had too much time to soften the slope. From Brock's perspective, extreme sports were all about calculated risks and common sense. Stupidity and plain old bad luck were what got people killed. Jay's feigned indifference was beginning to bug him.

"Brock, we couldn't ask for better conditions. This high-pressure system guarantees us a steep and radical descent," Jay said as he clicked into his board and pointed to the cloudless sky above them.

"Enough, Mr. Weather Channel. The glacier awaits us like a gleaming bride. Last one to the tent makes dinner!"

Brock whooped as he glided toward the edge and dropped into the vast powder bowl like a surfer barreling down a large wave.

Jay eased forward and watched Brock carve a series of long, smooth arcs, the tail of the snowboard throwing a powdery fan with each elegant turn. After seven or eight turns, Brock slowed to a stop about a thousand feet below. He burst out an ecstatic yelp and waved Jay on.

Amidst a backdrop of fourteen-thousand-foot granite peaks standing guard above him like stoic sentries, Jay bent his knees and started his vertical descent following a line similar to Brock's.

Keeping the nose of his board above the soft, powdery snow, Jay flew down the mountainside, hooting and hollering all the way. Setting up for a long frontside turn, he leaned toward the side of the mountain, body fully extended, his left hand skeetering across the snow. Jay crossed Brock's tracks three times, completing the unfinished half of what was becoming a series of figure eights. As he carved a thick slice through the fourth track, a loud, muffled rumble sounded like an explosive depth charge from underneath the snow's surface. Instantaneously, a jagged series of fissures crackled in a horizontal direction to the right and left above the snowboard's trail.

Three hundred yards below, Brock gasped as the mountain shook off a piece of itself—a tumultuous field of snow, ice, and rock roughly the size of a basketball court. Brock saw his friend glance back to see the cascading monster only fifty yards behind; his speed was his only advantage. Churning. Grinding. Spewing. Hurling. Roaring. The growing avalanche crashed down the steep slope pursuing Jay in a chaotic, thundering stampede.

The roar above Brock grew like a derailing freight train, with huge ice blocks the size of boxcars exploding down on each other. Smaller boulders the size of trash cans rocketed beyond the icy mass, strafing anything in their path below. Huge plumes of snow shot through the air like sky-rockets. Brock didn't waste a second more and thrust himself down the mountain, knowing his position on the hill was more precarious than Jay's. He tucked himself into a racer's stance and fled, not knowing if the icy maelstrom had already consumed Jay or if he was next to be packed in ice. His jaw set and firm, Brock never looked back.

Below him lay the open expanse of the Palisades Glacier in perfect stillness, the surrounding mountain peaks echoing the fury of nature's blast above. Racing at what had to be at least fifty miles an hour, Brock looked at the sun-drenched slope and hoped the softer snow below wouldn't hinder his speed. Jay caught up with him and pointed toward the yellow tent below, his words unintelligible against the roaring snow. The icy wind stinging their faces like a swarm of bees, the two tore down the mountain together.

Gradually, the gap widened between the monster and the two young men. Losing momentum as the slope flattened around the glacier's wide lower apron, the avalanche ground to a slow stop, its bellowing dying in the echoes above. Not far from the tent, Brock and Jay flopped on the slushy snow in their snowboards, panting and exhausted, sweating, gasping for air, half-laughing to be alive, still scared out of their minds for what could have been.

Back in the city, Jessica Matthews brushed her flowing brown hair away from her face and grabbed the black plastic whistle hanging on the red string around her neck. Inhaling, she paused and released a high-pitched shrill. Once more, she wet her lips and blew again.

"C'mon in! Recess is over," she hollered to the hundred or so kids on the Longfellow Elementary School playground. Like ants scurrying on the hot pavement, the children grabbed their jump ropes, red rubber balls, street hockey sticks, hula hoops, hopscotch bean bags, footballs, and Frisbees. There was one more cherry drop on the bars, an acrobatic dismount off the swings, and a final baby-bouncy slider against the handball wall. The playground equipment was put away—some of it just thrown in, other pieces put away neatly—in a faded yellow ball shed.

Like the pulsating, rhythmic motion of a caterpillar, a line of screaming, laughing kids queued behind the white porcelain drinking fountain. Shouts of "Stop pushing!" came from kids at the front of the line who acted as a buffer to protect the boy drinking from getting his teeth knocked out.

"Hurry up!" Jessica yelled. "Get a quick drink. Make sure everything's put away and head to class."

Running up to Jessica carrying a red handball, a small girl whose hair was cut in a short bob cried, "Mrs. Matthews! Mrs. Matthews! Stephen threw this ball in my face, and then he called me a dorfuss!"

"Is that so, Jenny?" Jessica asked as she knelt down next to her.

"*Yes!* And then he told me to put the ball away. I didn't check it out . . . he did," Jenny Smith exclaimed in the exasperated anguish of a second-grader.

"Okay, give the ball to me. I'll take care of this, and you scoot on to class."

"Thank you, Mrs. Matthews," Jenny said, who then gave her a quick hug and stuck her tongue out at Stephen Markowitz, who was now standing at the end of the drinking fountain line. Jenny hurried off to class and yelled over her shoulder, "You're in big trouble, Stephen Markowitz!"

Jessica looked at him and said, "Stephen, please come here right now."

After settling the textbook playground case of Smith versus Markowitz, Jessica walked over to the ball shed, straightened the tangled mess of jump ropes and balls, and locked it. As she headed to her second-grade class of twenty-three students, Jessica thought about the argument she had had with David the night before.

The two of them had hardly spent any time together in the past month. David had just recently entered the life insurance industry and was putting in long hours to develop new clients. Since nights were the best time to call and meet with people, evenings became a source of contention. He felt unappreciated and stressed about finances. She was lonely and felt unsupported in raising their two teenagers.

Jessica had tried to initiate a conversation about developing a schedule that would be mutually beneficial, but in less than a minute, David had blown up at her, asking her where she thought the money was going to come from to pay the mortgage, two car payments, taxes, food, utilities, and why they chose to live in such an expensive town. They had two incomes and were still struggling financially.

David had gone on and on until Jessica had finally burst into tears and the two of them had gone to bed without speaking to each other.

Today, she wondered how much that promise they had both made at church on Sunday meant to David. That time in the fellowship hall was so special, Jessica thought. She'd never seen Pastor Max so sincere; a tenderness came from him that was so different than his usual hard-charging personality. She sensed a real change in her pastor. She wished she could say the same about David.

Despite their argument, Jessica knew David loved her. He was just under so much pressure, much of which he put on himself, with the job transition and all. Things *were* tight right now, but not terribly so. Thankfully they hadn't racked up credit card debt like some of their friends. Once David got a few more clients under his belt, she was sure their schedule would get back to normal.

Jessica's mind then drifted to the issue of Scott. She could have nailed him Sunday morning for breaking curfew. When she woke up after midnight on Saturday night and saw his empty bedroom, she went down to the living room and read until one-thirty in the morning, frequently pausing to pray that Scott would come home safe.

After going back to bed, through a muffled fog of drowsiness, she heard Scott tell his father what time it was. Too tired to deal with it then, Jessica succumbed to sleep. But on Sunday morning, she did feel a little guilty for not telling David the truth about what time Scott really arrived home. She hated the idea of creating a big fight before church. Then, when they were in a flush of goodwill and excitement after church, she didn't have the heart to bring it up. She decided to deal with Scott on her own.

As she arrived at her classroom and walked into the brightly colored room filled with animal pictures, tempera paint artwork, science projects, hamster cages, world maps, craft tables, and four rows of neatly lined-up wood desks, Jessica's eye caught a bunch of red and green on her desk. Red roses.

In a beautiful glass vase, a dozen red roses accented with white baby's breath sat smack dab in the middle of her desk. Jessica smiled with a hint of embarrassment as she navigated the aisle to her desk, knowing what she was in for next.

A cackle of giggles erupted from little mouths as she plucked a small envelope from a clear, plastic fork. Jessica smiled and gave the kids an "Oh, you hush" wave of her hand. She opened the envelope and read the card:

I'm sorry. If Jesus had been married, I don't think he would have treated his wife like I did yesterday. You're the most important person to me in this whole world. I'll be home before six. Love, David.

On Friday morning, just before noon, Vic Gennaro led Max and Emilio Alvarez down the long center aisle in the Gennaro Leatherworks factory. The one-hundred-thousand-square-foot factory and adjacent shipping facility sat in the heart of L.A.'s garment district. On one side of the aisle, they heard the furious staccato tapping sound of dozens of sewing machines operated by older Hispanic women, their wrinkled hands deftly guiding the leather pieces into exquisite-looking purses, jackets, pants, and accessory items. Opposite the sewing machines were large, rectangular cutting tables. Here, men and women worked fast with razor-sharp blades cutting swatches of all sizes from plastic templates.

The factory was a flurry of activity. Since workers were paid by each piece they cut, sewed, stitched, or stacked, there was little talk among them except for an occasional yell for more buttons or new cutting blades. A few managers walked around with clipboards and walkie talkies checking inventories and lot sizes.

"Everything you see here," Vic began to explain to Max and Emilio, "is made by hand. The reason people keep buying our products again and again is because of the quality." Vic picked up a leather jacket at the end of one assembly line. "This jacket is the only leather jacket a person will ever need. See these seams here," he said pointing at the stitched line along the sleeve. "These seams are bombproof. I don't do any work overseas, so I pay a little more for labor— I'm not going to miss it. Why not help the local economy, especially when I've got the best workers in Los Angeles right here," Vic waved his hand, gesturing to the hundreds of people working with speed and initiative. "Many of my staff have been with me for years—whole families—I've hired cousins, aunts, uncles, sons, and daughters."

"How do your wages compare with the other clothing companies in L.A.?" Emilio asked, curious to gauge what it was really like to work here.

"Ask anyone in the garment district: I pay higher wages than any of my competitors. I expect superior work from my people and they are fairly compensated for it. Talk to Tony, my operations manager, and he'll tell you how many people come to the back door each week looking for work. Word gets out quickly when someone resigns or gets fired for sloppy work."

Vic led Max and Emilio through a door and into a large, drab room filled with over ten tables, chairs, and wood benches, with a few snack machines in the back. There was a thick, dank smell in the air and only a couple of windows to allow in a limited amount of sunlight. Vic flipped on the fluorescent lights, their whitish glow revealing gray walls splotched with scrapes and peeling plaster.

In an apologetic tone, Vic said, "I know it ain't pretty, but ever since we met in the fellowship hall and made that promise about asking what Jesus would do, my mind's been racing with ideas on how to make things better around here." Vic added, "If you think this is bad, you should see some of the other places downtown. My place isn't a sweatshop where people pass out from dying of heat. I do have heating for the winter and air-conditioning for the summer, but enough of that for now. What you talked about last week, Max, really got me thinking about the potential here for good, about everything that can be done to make these peoples' lives a little bit better."

Max looked around the room. *Yeah, this place does need a bit of work.* He turned to Vic and said, "That's great Vic, but were you serious when you said one of your employees leads a lunchtime Bible study with a hundred people? That's unheard of!"

With that, a loud whistle sounded from the factory floor announcing the noon lunch hour.

"See for yourself, Max," Vic gestured, "because here they come." Vic smiled as the workers poured through the lunchroom doors jockeying for their favorite tables.

Soon the room was packed with what appeared to be more than a hundred people busy opening lunch boxes and plastic containers filled with refried beans and tortillas. Women poured spicy salsa and fresh jalapenos into bowls. Some opened simple brown bags filled with sandwiches and fruit. An incessant chatter of Spanish and English filled the lunchroom like a late afternoon Dodger game.

Vic placed one hand on Max's shoulder, the other on Emilio's and said, "I want to give these people more than a better work environment; I want to give them something that will nourish their lives. Many of these people have second jobs they work on the weekend and they don't have time to go to church. Some of them are so busy providing for their families that they don't have time for church activities or Bible studies or anything like that. Word got out that the two of you would be here today, and others were drawn by the flyers posted in the lunchroom. Max, I'd like you to tell them about everything that's happened at First Church the past couple weeks and how that led up to the promise of asking 'What would Jesus do?'" Vic turned and looked at Emilio. "I think Max's message would run on about two cylinders if you weren't here, Emilio. If you could translate for Max, I'm sure these people would appreciate hearing his story in their own language."

Max was dumbfounded. Speaking on the fly was never his strength. He always prepared for his messages by making meticulous notes. He'd also never spoken to a blue-collar group before, much less one that didn't speak his language. He didn't know their customs and culture, let alone what would be relevant to them. And what could this group possibly want to hear from him? Sure, he'd taken a cross-cultural ministry class in seminary, but this was different. Max's stomach felt queasy as blood began to drain from his face.

Vic saw the uneasiness on Max's face and laughed. "Come on, Pastor; they're not going to bite you. Just do what Jesus did and tell 'em a story!" Emilio joined in the laughter as Vic pushed the two in the center of the room and motioned for Emilio to introduce themselves.

Emilio spoke above the din and waved his hand to catch everyone's attention. *"Hermanos en Cristo, es un gran placer estar aqui con vosostros en este dia."*

As the lunch crowd quieted, a sea of serious faces stared at Max and Emilio. Hearing Emilio's words, Max felt desperately inadequate and full of anxiety. The room was warm with so many bodies. Max's forehead began to perspire. He nervously wiped it and faintly smiled to the countless sets of dark eyes before him. His mouth felt dry. Pasty. He felt like an immense, radiating spotlight was trained on him like a prisoner caught in a jailbreak.

Through Emilio's rhythmic Latin accent, Max heard his name mentioned. Emilio nodded and gave him the okay to begin.

Max took a quick breath and whispered a silent prayer. His Spanish wasn't that rusty, he figured, so why not try to build a bridge and say something in their language?

He wanted to relate to these people in some way, even if it was the most basic of greetings. Max began by saying hello and telling the crowd he had just had lunch himself, a ham sandwich in fact.

Before Max could utter another word, the crowd burst into hysterics, the tremendous roar of laughter hitting him like a reverberating shockwave. Across the room, white teeth flashed and eyes lit up as people clapped their hands, slapped each others' backs, and bent over in comic pain.

A few older women tried to show some restraint and respect, but after a few seconds, they too were swept away by the hilarity of Max's words.

"Wha-wha-what is it?" Max stammered. "What did I say wrong?"

Emilio was no help. He was in stitches like the rest of them. His red-lined eyes filled with tears, Emilio could barely get the words out, "You . . . you . . . you said that you had a soap sandwich for lunch!"

"A soap sandwich?" Max questioned. "I said a ham sandwich!"

"No, no, no, Max," Emilio corrected. "You said *jabon*, not *jamon*."

A small smile broke the tension on Max's face as he realized how badly he'd just slaughtered his introduction. Soon he was laughing as hard as everyone else in the lunchroom. Emilio finally quieted the crowd again, but not before Max received a final round of applause and loud whistles.

Relaxed now, Max began telling the story of Jack Manning in a simple and clear voice, the steps that led to changes in his own life and in a number of lives at First Church. As Emilio translated every few sentences, Max went on to talk about the importance of work and how all people are looking for meaning and satisfaction in their lives. Max told the crowd that they are a reflection of God's handiwork and how God designed them to reflect his goodness here on earth. He spoke about how the quality of a person's work is a reflection of their own character and how every person can develop their character by looking at the life of Jesus Christ. He then went on to explain the question he put before the people of First Church.

"We would all benefit by asking ourselves 'What would Jesus do?' before making any decision that impacts others," Max said to his attentive audience. "It doesn't matter who you are or what you do. This is a simple question that will make a profound difference in your work, in your families, and in your friendships."

After speaking for about twenty minutes, Max turned it over to Emilio, who closed the meeting with a short prayer and a word of thanks for their time. There was a light round of applause and a few orders for soap sandwiches, which Max waved off with a laugh.

Max finally breathed a sigh of relief and motioned for Vic, who was leaning against the back wall with a smirk on his face.

Vic came forward and announced his renovation plans for the lunchroom, which elicited a robust round of cheers and hoots. That wasn't all, Vic said, and told them to be on the lookout for more changes coming in the near future.

After shaking many hands, the three walked to Emilio's car in the parking lot. As Max and Emilio got in, Vic asked, "So, Max, what'd you think?"

"First," Max started, "it went better than I expected, but I think—no, I know—you owe Emilio and me lunch for setting us up like that. Second, I'm only coming back when you get that lunchroom cleaned up," Max joked. "Third . . ."

Emilio cut in. "And I'll bring the soap sandwiches!"

The three laughed as Vic leaned into the window and pointed to Emilio. "Take your gringo friend home and give him some Spanish lessons, will ya? And make sure to bring him back in a week, okay?"

Max's cries of feigned protest were drowned out as Emilio nodded in agreement and pulled away from the curb.

5

On Saturday morning, Jessica Matthews stood at the kitchen stove making pancakes. Scott sat at the breakfast room table reading the sports section, and Kelly, still dressed in her robe and pajamas, read a skateboard magazine. David slept in, catching up on some much-needed sleep.

"Scott, you know I've been busy with parent/teacher conferences this week, but I've been meaning to ask you about your lip. What happened?" Jessica asked as she walked around the counter and flipped three more pancakes on his plate.

"Whattaya mean? What does it look like I did?" he replied defensively.

Scott stabbed another forkful and glared at Kelly.

"Listen, young man. I asked you a simple question and I don't appreciate your tone of voice. How did you get that cut on your lip?"

"Somebody left their stupid skateboard at the top of the stairs the other night, and I tripped over it," he said, his voice rising to get Kelly's attention. "I could've been killed!"

Jessica looked over at Kelly, who now had an "oops-here-it-comes" expression on her face. "Kelly, how many times have I told you to keep that skateboard in the garage? You know it's dangerous to leave it at the top of the stairs."

"Yeah, you idiot!"

"Shut up, Scott!" Kelly hissed and then lobbed her own offense. "By the way, what *time* did you trip on my skateboard the other night?"

Jessica put down her spatula and stood between the two snarling siblings. "Alright, both of you, that's enough! Scott, take your plate and go eat at the counter. Kelly, you stay here. And if I hear another word out of either of you, you'll both be grounded this weekend."

Scott's eyes burned at Kelly as he picked up his plate and sat on a stool at the kitchen counter. Neither of them said a word. They both knew Mom was serious.

A few minutes of tense silence passed until Kelly spoke. "Mom, I'm stuffed. Can I go to my room and get ready for soccer?"

"Yes, dear, and don't forget to straighten your bed." *Good,* she thought, *this will give me a few minutes with Scott.*

Jessica walked to the counter where Scott sat quietly eating his breakfast, carefully chewing each bite. She finally had the chance to talk with him alone.

"Scott, what time did you get in last Saturday night?"

"Dad knows. Ask him."

"I'm not asking your father, Scott. I'm asking you. What time did you get in?"

"Just before twelve." Scott didn't dare look his mom in the eyes.

"Oh, really," Jessica mused. "Just before twelve. Is that right?"

"Yeah, that's right."

"Explain to me then, when I woke up at twelve-thirty, how was it that the hall light was still on and your bed was empty?"

Scott played with the syrup on his plate with his fork and responded, "Okay, I got home late. A little after one. A couple of the guys needed a ride home. What was I supposed to do? Leave them stranded?"

Jessica straightened her back, her face becoming flush. "Scott Matthews! I can't believe you're lying right to my face. When I woke up and saw you weren't home yet, I went down to the living room and read until one-thirty in the morning." Her voice raised. "Look me in the eye, young man. You were not home a little after one!"

Her glare met him forcefully. In a defeated voice, he said, "Two A.M. I swear it wasn't any later than two."

"Scott?" Jessica cried in near anguish. "What about all those talks we had a few weeks ago? About your curfew? Your attitude around the house? Don't you care about how your father and I feel?"

"Me care? I'm not the problem. He's the one that's never around. Ever since he changed jobs, he doesn't have time for anybody but himself. All he ever does now is work. If he can't keep his promises, then why do I have to keep mine about being home on time?"

"Scott, your father works very hard for all of us. You know that it wasn't his choice to lose his job; you can't hold that against him."

"Yeah, well why not?" Scott yelled in a defensive voice. "He used to come to all my games, but now all he does is say that he'll *try* to make my games, but then never shows."

"Scott, this is serious. I'm going to have to tell your father you broke curfew. We had an agreement about this."

Scott knew he'd be in big trouble for breaking curfew a third time. Dad had been pretty stressed out lately too. That wouldn't help either. He bolted out of his chair and pleaded,

"No, Mom! I'm sorry I lied to you. I messed up. I won't do it again. Just don't tell Dad, *pleeease!*"

Jessica felt stuck. Caught between loyalty to her husband and love for her son, she knew Scott's anger had been building the past couple of months over David's repeated broken promises to make his basketball games. David just didn't have time for the kids like he used to—he was working so hard to get ahead in this new job. She knew it wasn't right for him to break his promises, but she also understood the pressure he was under. Jessica looked at Scott and closed her eyes for a moment, asking God for wisdom to know what to do next.

"I think I know the solution to this problem," a deep voice sounded from the hallway as David appeared in the kitchen doorway.

"Dad!" Scott gulped, half surprised, half in fear of what was coming next.

"Dave, you're up. We were just talking about you," Jessica joined in, casting a quick glance at Scott.

Scott felt himself beginning to crumble. His dad's wrath was coming for sure, and he was only moments away from being grounded for life.

Dressed in blue jeans and a red flannel shirt, David walked across the kitchen, placed his hands on Scott's shoulders, and cleared his throat.

Scott didn't know what to do. He wondered for a second if he should cower or stand up to his dad by telling him exactly what he told his mom.

"Scott," David began with a slight quiver in his voice, his eyes becoming watery. "I owe you a big apology. A number of apologies, in fact. I promised to make it to your basketball games, and I haven't come to a single one yet. I haven't been a man of my word, and I've earned your disrespect as a result of it. This past week, I've realized how I've been shortchanging you, your mother, and Kelly by putting my job ahead of my family, and I'm sorry, truly sorry, for hurting you. Will you forgive me?"

Scott's eyes were as wide as his mouth was open. He'd never heard his dad speak like that before. He broke curfew, and his dad was apologizing to him?

"Yeah, Dad . . . uh . . . yeah, sure."

"Thanks, son. Those are words I needed to hear." David smiled as he pulled Scott close to his chest.

Jessica stood next to the stove with one hand on her cheek, astonished at the words she'd just heard. Tears streamed down her face as she whispered a quiet prayer of thanks to God.

Scott returned his dad's hearty hug and thumped him on the back. Pulling away, he asked, "Dad, does this mean I'm not in trouble for breaking curfew?"

David looked over to Jessica, who threw her hands up in the air.

"Well, son, that's something your mom and I are going to have to talk about, but let's just say this for now: If I can start keeping my promises to you, will you be willing to keep your promises to us?"

"That sounds like something I can handle."

"Good, then that's the place where we both need to start."

Max stood at the pulpit on Sunday morning and looked at his congregation from a new perspective. The church was more crowded than it had been the past two weeks. Before, a full house would have seized Max with excitement, energizing him to deliver the dynamic messages he was known for. Today, however, his heart and mind weren't distracted by body counts or how the audience would respond to his jokes or his polished delivery. His heart finally felt at peace. Earlier in the week, he'd met with a counselor for help with the conflicting feelings he was still having over Jack's death. Jack was dead. Gone. Max couldn't change that, the counselor said. What he could do, the counselor suggested, was write Jack a good-bye letter, telling him how sorry he was for what happened and how he wished he would have treated him better. "I know that may sound strange, Max," the counselor said, "but forgiveness isn't for dead people . . . only the living."

All week long, in between counseling First Church members who'd accepted the promise the previous Sunday, individually talking with elders about proposed changes for First Church, answering questions from concerned members who thought Max was reacting to Jack Manning's death in a bizarre manner, and talking with Jack's brother in New Mexico about how Ashley was handling her father's death, the overriding question for Max's upcoming sermon was, "What would Jesus say to this church?"

Max's initial thoughts about this question scared him because he knew Jesus wasn't shy about blasting hypocrisy. Especially in the church. His other primary concern, at least at first, was what would people think or say about him? He was usually so sensitive to people's comments after the service and, sometimes, outright defensive when someone challenged him on a particular point. Max wasn't convinced that his sometimes temperamental nature had changed much. There were so many aspects of the promise he made that remained untested.

But as he reviewed the notes he'd written a few days ago about what Jesus would do in First Church, a surge of confidence welled up in him as he felt the assurance of the Spirit's leading. In humility and love, his role as a pastor was to lead, guide, nurture, defend, and gently discipline his flock according to biblical truth. Max could now see how he had earlier shirked his responsibility to preach the whole Word of God and not simply those selections that would inspire or comfort the hearts of those at First Church. *We really are like sheep,* Max thought to himself. *If we only eat and sleep, then we get fat and lazy.* If someone really wanted to follow the Master, a serious engagement between the selfish nature and the Spirit of God was to be expected. Walking in the steps of Jesus required the practical demonstration of faith seen in works of mercy and compassion, action and obedience. Could followers of Jesus really claim to be disciples if they weren't willing to make the personal sacrifices that come with that confession?

Outside, before the service started, Max overheard people wondering out loud what this week's service would be like. His ears caught the words of one woman who was astonished to find out that he'd visited Vic Gennaro's garment workers on Friday. Another person mentioned the chaos of the past two Sundays and how a few prominent families had left First Church in a huff. Max didn't let the chatter and hubbub over the changes sweeping First Church rattle him. With deep certainty, he now refused to allow the whims of public opinion to shape today's message.

As Max delivered his sermon, the members of First Church were hearing him, for the first time, preach against religious hypocrisy and the deceitfulness of wealth. Looking at the text of Deuteronomy 8, Max outlined how common it was for people of all generations to receive the material blessings of God only to then forget him and his commands.

"You may say to yourself," Max said, "'My power and the strength of my hands have produced this wealth for me.' But remember the Lord your God, for it is he who gives you the ability to produce wealth."

There was nothing hostile or self-righteous about Max's tone. He spoke with the same tenderness and simplicity of last week, although his stammering and disheveled appearance were noticeably absent. Most who heard his words sensed his sincerity and his desire to help everyone in the crowded church live lives of visible and authentic faith. His new stance on the abuse of wealth, our quickness to abandon God, and the repugnance of religious hypocrisy was clear and uncompromising.

Max closed the service by inviting others to make the promise of asking "What would Jesus do?" in their daily lives for the next year. Whether one made the promise the previous week or today, all were invited for a short meeting to be held after the service in the fellowship hall.

Rikki Winslow offered a flawless solo that ended the service on an upbeat note. She did notice earlier, though, that during Pastor Max's sermon her mother seemed particularly fidgety.

Afterward, the fellowship hall had even more people in it than the week before. There had to be close to a hundred people in the room. First Church members of all ages and even a few folks Max didn't recognize sat at the round tables, on the couches, and leaned along the bricks lining the fireplace. Near to where Max stood, about twenty or so high school kids sat on the floor with their legs crossed. Max even noticed a few elders and other influential people who led the various church committees.

Max greeted everyone and said how exciting it was to see so many people with such a fervent desire to follow Christ. He asked Vic to open the meeting with prayer, which Vic did by thanking God for his grace and goodness. In a quiet voice, Vic also prayed that God would give each person in the room the wisdom to know how to follow Christ each day in the coming week. As Vic closed, Rikki Winslow began to sing the doxology in a reverent, engaging tone.

> Praise God, from whom all blessings flow;
> praise him, all creatures here below;

Soon, the whole room joined her.

> praise him above, ye heavenly host;
> praise Father, Son, and Holy Ghost.
> Amen.

As it had been the previous week, today's fellowship was earnest and heartfelt. Each person present wanted to encourage and strengthen one another. For the newcomers, the Spirit's presence was obvious from the expressed depth of emotion and genuine worship coming from each person in the hall.

Max reviewed the details of the one-year promise, which weren't complicated and took only a few minutes to explain. He then opened the floor to the questions and dilemmas people faced in carrying out the promise they had made.

Jessica Matthews started by explaining the conflicts she faced in her parent/teacher conferences. Some parents, whose children were not performing particularly well in school, had banded together to criticize her teaching style. Her initial reaction, which she restrained, was to fight back and tell the parents to take a flying leap onto the 110 Freeway. Instead, she tried to look at the situation from the parents' perspective and discovered that even though the parents weren't right about forming a lynch mob, they were probably just worried about their children getting behind. She went on to explain how she developed a plan with each of the parents to help their children's progress.

"Asking what Jesus would do wasn't easy because it meant making a clear choice not to react when I was being attacked, but I was able to arrive at a solution with the parents I may not have otherwise come to," Jessica summarized.

"But what about when nobody's coming at you," Gina Page jumped in. "I have a friend who works at a coffeehouse; he's so disillusioned about life. He's constantly down on himself, and if there's anyone I could think of who doesn't have hope or a sense of purpose in life, it would be him. He doesn't believe in God or any religion for that matter. His family's all messed up, and I can tell he's bitter about his life. How can I know what Jesus would do when I can't even figure out what's the best way for him to help himself?"

"Sometimes you can't know, Gina," Max offered. "The best thing to do is to be his friend. That's what Jesus was, a friend to sinners like all of us in this room. A lot of times, people *aren't* looking for answers; they're looking for people to love and accept them just the way they are. Then, when they begin to feel secure, they are willing to evaluate your life and see if the answer you've found is real or not."

Paul Wickman explained the trouble he was having in making investment decisions with companies whose policies and practices he didn't agree with. He also mentioned his aborted attempt to talk with his wife about the promise he made. She described this promise business as a bit too extreme for her and wouldn't hear another word of it.

David Matthews told the group how he was struggling to trust God with his family's financial situation and how he was previously mortgaging his family relationships by enslaving himself to his work. He decided this week to cut back on work, but the trust part wasn't coming easy. He didn't know where the money would come from, but his decision was worth it primarily because he and his son had been reconciled.

Scott, who decided to come to the fellowship hall this morning and was seated with the other high school students, stood up and told the group how he had decided to stop drinking. He said he finally realized how his stupid decisions were hurting his whole family. Scott closed by pointing to his father and saying he was grateful to God for giving him a dad who was man enough to admit when he was wrong.

Vic Gennaro stood up and in his fast-paced Italian manner described the warm reception Max and Emilio received when Max shared his story with the lunch Bible study group at Gennaro Leatherworks. He got a big laugh out of everyone in the fellowship hall when he explained Max's penchant for soap sandwiches.

A few other people stood and commented on how they were reflecting on the seriousness of the question in their lives. Everyone in the room agreed that even though the question was simple, even easy to ask, the implications and consequences of following through on the promise bumped each person out of their comfort zone. Asking what Jesus would do required a deeper knowledge of God, a deeper desire to pray before acting, and a more serious reflection about the Christ found in Scripture than they had been used to before.

Max closed the meeting with prayer. Afterward, some people decided to continue their discussions by meeting for lunch at a restaurant on Colorado Boulevard. Others made breakfast appointments for later in the week to pray with and encourage one another.

Although they were a few years apart in age, Gina and Rikki were friendly and eager to talk about the riveting events happening at First Church and in their own lives. Gina invited Rikki to lunch at her home in San Marino.

As Gina pulled into the long, gated driveway from Virginia Avenue in her emerald-green BMW, the house wasn't immediately visible. Rikki had been here a few times before, but each time the enormous Mediterranean-style, red-tiled roof home came into view, she was awed by the fact that only three people lived there.

The front lawn, arguably the size of a small park, was lined with colorful flower beds filled with azaleas and long rows of purple petunias. From a large white gazebo at the far corner of the lawn hung round clay pots filled with pink and red impatiens. The sweeping arc of a grand magnolia tree cast soft shadows on a portion of the grass. On the left side of the home, an elaborate web of bougainvillea nearly reached the second story, its paper-thin petals radiating a spectacular flourish of burgundy red.

As Gina sped along the lengthy driveway, Rikki could see the tall pine trees in the backyard, which she knew held a tennis court, swimming pool, chipping green, rose garden, freshwater koi ponds, and a spacious swim house that also served as an entertainment center for barbecues and small parties.

The Page mansion was a far cry from the small, two-bedroom condominium Rikki shared with her mom in Pasadena, but Rikki wasn't one to complain about the consequences of her parents' divorce. Her mother worked hard, not only as an executive secretary, but also in developing Rikki's singing career. To pay for singing lessons and the studio time necessary to create demo tapes, Valerie Winslow arranged for Rikki to sing at church services, special events, and weddings in Southern California. The two of them didn't have much in a material sense, but Rikki was content with what she had.

After parking outside the four-car garage, Gina and Rikki entered the back door and went into the kitchen. At the large, rectangular island in the middle of the kitchen stood Florence, Gina's aunt, who was cutting celery, red bell peppers, and romaine lettuce for a salad. Overhead was a smattering of large and small pots, colanders, silver utensils of all shapes and sizes, strings of garlic, and bunches of decorative red chili peppers.

"You're right on time," Florence greeted the two girls. "I'm almost finished with the salad."

"Aunt Florence, you remember my friend Rikki Winslow, don't you?" Gina asked, introducing her.

"Remember her? How could I forget that lovely voice from church . . . that is, when I make it out of bed on Sundays. How you doing, sweetheart?"

"I'm doing well, Miss Page. Thank you for asking," Rikki responded politely.

The sister of Gina's father, Florence Page had never married. When Gina's parents died in the plane crash in Colorado, Florence took custody of Brock and Gina, only nine and eight at the time of the accident. Before his death, Gina's father had been the owner of Stagecoach Bank. The largest bank in California, it had been founded by his great-grandfather during the California goldrush in the late 1800s. Gina's father had established a sizable, separate trust for his children in the event that anything ever happened to him and their mother.

Now in her fifties, Florence spent the majority of her time managing the family's considerable assets and investments. She was an astute businesswoman and involved herself in many of San Marino's social activities and clubs. Though she could be endearing and warm when the situation warranted, she was also strong-willed and opinionated. A fierce proponent of equal rights, she had lobbied hard and spent thousands of dollars to gain entrance to the exclusive San Marino Men's Club, her repeated attempts still unsuccessful.

A few minutes later, the three sat around a glass table on the patio. As Florence poured large glasses of iced tea, she asked Rikki, "How is that contract coming for the CD you're going to record this summer?"

A forkful of salad almost in her mouth, Rikki stopped and said, "Oh, I didn't know you knew about the contract. I don't mean to sound put-offish, but I've only told a couple friends about it."

"Don't be silly, girl," Florence gestured. "I bump into your mom almost every week in town. She's the one who can't stop talking about it. She told me that you have three or four companies chasing after you, begging you to sign with them. She even hinted that you may get a six-figure contract. That's certainly not pocket change for a first deal, but I'd pay money to hear you sing."

"*Aunt Florence,*" Gina grimaced. "Rikki's recording contract and their finances are none of our business. Let the poor girl alone. She came here to have lunch, not to play 'Twenty Questions' about her singing career."

"I was just asking," Florence replied with a smirk and a roll of her eyes at Gina.

"If I were you," a fourth voice broke in from the kitchen, "I'd squeeze every penny I could outta those companies. Hold out for a million. Make 'em get on their knees."

"Brock, what are you doing home so soon?" Gina asked in a surprised voice.

Leaning against the patio door with a bottle of Corona beer in his hand, Gina's older brother stood looking muscular and confident. He was wearing a baggy ski jacket, black Levi's, and a raccoon-eye sunburn pattern etched on his handsome face.

Oooh . . . is he cute, Rikki thought to herself.

"I got tired of boarding up at Mammoth and the Palisades, so I went up to Tahoe. When no new storms came in, I decided to come home for a few days."

"So, where are you headed next, Captain Adventure?" Florence joked as Brock gave her a kiss on the forehead.

"I'm glad you asked. Probably to Joshua Tree next week. There're some new routes I want to climb." Brock smiled and sat down in an empty chair. "How 'ya doing, Rikki?"

"Fine, Brock. How are you?"

"Well, after almost getting killed by an avalanche, I'd say I'm doing pretty good."

"Avalanche?" Gina spoke up, her tone clearly doubting Brock's claim.

"I'm *serious*. Jay and I were in the Palisades, and we got chased by a wall of snow and rocks and ice bigger than this house."

"Oh, Brock," Gina teased. "You always come back from your travels around the world with these larger-than-life fish stories. Let's see . . . there was the tiger shark that bit your surfboard in half on the north shore of Hawaii . . . there were those guys in Mexico who robbed you with machetes at the pyramids. What about alien abductions? How come you haven't been abducted like Elvis yet?"

The three women laughed as Brock raised his arms in defeat and swore that the avalanche story was true.

"Rikki has been telling us about her recording contract," Florence said, picking up where the conversation left off.

"Well actually, Miss Page, I have been thinking about the contract a lot lately. Though we haven't signed with any particular company yet, I'm beginning to question if I should even pursue a professional singing career. I'm wondering if that is where God is really leading me."

"You'd better not tell your mother about that," Florence cautioned. "She's got big plans for you, you know. Look at all the people you could touch with your music. Why would you consider abandoning your singing when you are right on the verge of a breakthrough that other people would die for?"

Rikki sat up in her chair and looked Florence Page directly in the eye. "Because, at least for me, I'm not sure that's what Jesus would do."

"You don't mean to tell me you're taking that First Church promise business so seriously," Florence chided, the patronizing words of her voice sounding like an old headmistress. "I've seen religious fads come and go. Can't you see this whole promise deal is Max Henry's emotional reaction to that homeless person's death?"

"Aunt Florence," Gina broke in. "It's not just an emotional reaction to Jack Manning's death! It's a question worth asking for every person who goes to church. Why do you think so many people criticize the church and God and religion? It's because hardly anyone lives out what they say they believe. It's because nobody's passionate about anything anymore. If Christians aren't going to think and act and live like Christ, then what makes them any different from a vegetarian or an environmentalist or someone chanting for world peace?"

"I'm sorry to excuse myself," Brock said as he stood up to go back in the kitchen, "but this conversation's getting a little too heavy for me. I prefer watching the Lakers battle the Celtics."

Florence Page's eyes cut a razor-sharp stare across the table to Gina. "Asking what Jesus would do is a pointless question. It's impractical and unrealistic to think that anyone can know the mind of Christ two thousand years after his death. How is anyone supposed to know what Jesus would do in today's world? We only know what he did long ago. Are you going to drive down to the City of Hope and start healing terminally ill people? Isn't that what Jesus would do?" she asked sarcastically.

Gina felt a surge of emotion rising in her blood. Aunt Florence just didn't get it. How could she when going to church was about as important to her as going to the dry cleaner? Both of them were as angry as they ever got at each other, but Gina knew her aunt's temper was kept in check by Rikki's presence.

"Asking what Jesus would do," Rikki said calmly, "isn't something that I take lightly. It's a serious question that can't be based on emotion or a spiritual fad people flock to, like wearing bracelets or necklaces with crosses. It's a question that must be answered with a lot of prayer and the Holy Spirit's help."

"That's exactly what I'm talking about," Florence blurted out. "Whenever I hear 'Holy Spirit this' and 'Holy Spirit that,' people start getting all emotional and acting like holy rollers. I'm a lot older than you two. You'll see this whole thing die down in a few weeks." Florence shook her head with one of her authoritative "so there!" looks on her face.

"Don't mean to be disrespectful, Aunt Flo," Gina said with a pert smile. "But one year is a lot longer than a few weeks, and that's how long we intend to keep our promise."

Florence stood up in a bit of a huff, but not before knocking her knee against the leg of the glass table. Throwing down her napkin, she picked up her plate. "Well, young lady," she said in a tight, clipped voice, "you are being disrespectful and more than a little arrogant, I'd say. You aren't acting the least bit Christian to me, and if you can't with your own family, why try with the rest of the world?"

Florence stormed off into the kitchen, her plate sent crashing into the sink. Gina and Rikki grimaced at each other for a second, then burst into laughter.

"Looks like you've got some salvage work to do, Gina."

"Oh, Aunt Florence will be fine. I'll apologize to her later; sometimes she just gets on my nerves. She always has to be right and know more than everyone else because she's older. She's wound tighter than a ball of string."

"I know. That's exactly how my mom's been lately with this whole record deal."

"What are you going to tell her, Rikki? Are you serious that you may drop the recording project?"

"Like I said, I'm not sure yet. I know there's money in my voice and that my mom is counting on it, but whose life are we talking about? I'm tired of feeling like I'm her only hope. My mom's going to go ballistic if I tell her I don't want to do it, but I'm becoming really disillusioned with the whole Christian music industry. The people we've been working with seem more concerned about money than ministering to people. I know it's not that way for every singer or musician in the industry, but I'm seriously questioning my motives for wanting a recording deal. Is it to be famous? Is it to have a lot of money—more than we need—so Mom and I can feel secure? Is it to help and inspire people to love God? What is it? I'm not sure I know yet."

"You know, I've been thinking similar things lately about all the money I've been blessed with. I'm beginning to wonder if it's really a curse. Everyone wants to be wealthy, but money seems to screw up people more than it does to better them or anyone else's lives! What purpose is there in spending my whole life pursuing pleasure and luxury, whether for myself or in the interior design career I've chosen?"

The two girls were silent for a moment as they pondered the implications of such questions. As they finished their salads and iced tea, Rikki and Gina resolved to pray for one another and continue down the course set before them, hoping to discover the answers to their questions along the way.

In the weeks and months that followed that first Sunday when Max Henry challenged his congregation to walk in the steps of Christ, the implications of that simple promise resulted in many sleepless nights, agonizing decisions, and long moments of self-examination. People began to examine their motives, their words, their wills. Selfishness, materialism, lust, covetousness, gossip, pride, and greed were just a few of the many offenses brought before the cleansing and regeneration of God's Spirit. Every person who had made the promise discovered, in one way or another, that with the promise came a cost. Regardless, the ultimate cost for everyone involved the daily denial of self. For all, the promise to ask what Jesus would do required a daily attentiveness to God's Spirit's in each and every decision.

Gradually, a sense of anticipation and momentum began to build. Bold ideas ignited a new passion among individuals to serve the needs of others in their careers and homes and communities through deeds of service and compassion. Many First Church members remarked how this new wave of enthusiasm and love for God was manifesting itself through simple, visible acts of goodness on Sunday morning and throughout the week.

The promise had taken root, but not without struggle or heartache. Like raising the bar in a high-jump competition, the tension of actually doing what Jesus would do was heightened in the conflicts that lay ahead.

6

he ebbing twilight cast long dark lines through the vertical mini-blinds in the heavy stillness of Candice's dorm room. On the bed, Candice clutched a pillow, her body in a fetal position, knees tucked close to her chest. Warm tears streamed down her cheeks as fear and confusion raced through her mind like a pair of taunting evil twins.

A small sliver of light snuck into the darkened bedroom from the bathroom. On the bathroom counter near the sink lay a small plastic stick with a rectangular window in the middle of it. In the center of the window was a red circle. It was the same red circle that was marked "positive" on the small cardboard box of the pregnancy test kit that rested on the slate-colored tile floor.

Earlier that week, Candice had experienced bouts of nausea in the morning and at different times throughout the day. She'd tried taking some medicine, thinking that she'd caught one of those viruses everyone was coming down with. When nothing else seemed to work, she went to the school infirmary and met with a kind doctor who poked around a little and finally said she knew what she thought the problem was.

The doctor inquired about Candice's personal life and asked if she was sexually active. Candice blurted no, which wasn't exactly true. At least, for right now, no, she was not sexually active and didn't even have a boyfriend. The doctor made herself a bit more clear.

"Have you been sexually active in the past two or three months?"

Sheepishly, Candice replied, "Well . . . um . . . yes. My boyfriend and I were close. Sexually, that is, but we took precautions."

"Did you ever have unprotected sex?"

Candice exhaled through her lower lip, her breath flipping her bangs upward. She began to grow nervous, knowing where this conversation was leading. "A couple times . . . yes."

The doctor didn't lecture. She asked Candice if she wanted to take a pregnancy test here in the office or if she wanted to take one home. Candice didn't want to stick around for a minute longer for fear of anyone seeing her. She asked for a kit and jammed it in her purse as if it was a bomb ready to explode.

As she was leaving, the doctor gave her two cards. The first was her own. She told Candice to call if she had any questions or needed further assistance. The second card listed the name and phone number of a downtown clinic where Candice could go if she wanted to terminate the pregnancy. The clinic was small and discreet—reasonably priced—and didn't attract much attention from the pro-lifers who marched on the sidewalks near the larger clinics in Los Angeles. The doctor said that she'd referred many girls to this same clinic, which performed very safe and effective procedures. These students, she said, went back to their studies and work in no time.

Candice left the infirmary feeling sick to her stomach, and she knew it wasn't because of morning sickness.

"Okay, what's the batting order for today?" Paul Wickman asked in a crisp, upbeat voice to the mass of loyal analysts and traders surrounding his desk.

"Intel is up a point for the day," barked a young man wearing round, tortoise-shell glasses. "This quarter's earnings exceeded last year's by 15 percent. Next generation chip due out next month."

"Okay, let's increase our position by fifty thousand shares. Let's get a move on that before it jumps any higher," Paul commanded and motioned toward a woman with short brown hair in front of him.

"Andrews Enterprises just signed a five-year, thirty-million-dollar contract with South Korea. Other contracts with countries in Africa and the Middle East are forthcoming. Their earnings are positioned to go through the roof once the ink is wet on those deals. Recommend a buy."

When Paul countered to hold Millennium's position as is, a buzz stirred about the room by the now puzzled portfolio management team.

Hold? Paul Wickman loved that company! Six weeks ago he couldn't stop talking about them. He always said war was good for the economy.

"Excuse me, Paul." Another woman raised her voice. "I don't think I'm the only one in the room who's wondering *why* you would issue a hold on Andrews."

Paul walked around to the front of his desk and sat on one corner. "Andrews does have remarkable earnings and their long-term potential is strong. We all know the core of their products are based in the U.S. aerospace industry, but recently, I've had serious ethical concerns with some of their subsidiaries, namely Protech. Protech is the largest U.S. supplier of landmines to foreign countries, and one of the chief end-users of their product are children who step on them.

I can't believe in good conscience that our investors would knowingly invest their money with such a firm."

"But aren't our investors' chief concerns high dividends, capital gains, and the overall growth of this fund?" an older man in a white shirt and a teal-speckled tie rebutted.

What ensued was a lengthy debate on the investing philosophy of the Millennium Fund. A discussion like this was quite out of the ordinary. Paul usually frowned on any conversation that lasted more than a minute or two while the market was open. His remarks unsettled a number of those on the team. Many of Paul's analysts and traders had aggressively interviewed for a position at Millennium because of his reputation as an outstanding fund manager. When had there ever been a debate on making moral and ethical investment decisions at Millennium? People cared about the Dow Jones and their retirement income, not invisible corporate entities hidden under the umbrella of multi-billion-dollar, worldwide conglomerates. This was Wall Street, not the Vatican.

By the end of the day, Paul was exhausted. Dozens of the most current analyst's reports lay on his desk screaming for attention before the Street opened tomorrow. After pouring himself a cup of bitter, black coffee, he checked his mailbox and found a slender letter addressed to him from the SEC, the United States Securities and Exchange Commission.

At his desk, Paul opened the envelope and read two short paragraphs that outlined a series of allegations by the SEC against a number of staff members at the Millennium Star Fund. The charges alleged a pattern of substantially large and suspect trades in their personal accounts following a large block purchase or sale of stock by one of the many companies held in the Millennium Star Fund. If such stock movements were found to be insider trades and thus illegal, the SEC warned that criminal charges would be pursued.

The letter directed Paul to first consult the Millennium's legal counsel and then to respond to the charges in writing within one week. A date was set for a formal meeting at the Millennium Fund offices in Los Angeles, whereby SEC investigators would begin formal investigative interviews with each staff member named in the letter. Paul's name was not mentioned, but for right now, that was the least of his concerns. Closing the blinds to separate his office from view of the trading pit and the myriad of cubicles, Paul sat back down at his desk, buried his face in his arms, and began to pray.

On the first Thursday in March, Don Marsh was busy setting up a colorful new display of gift coffees and chocolate biscotti dipping cookies at Starbucks. The new line of products boasted enticing exotic names from faraway destinations: *Wild Sumatran, Ethiopian Sulawasi, Guatemala Antigua,* and *Yukon Gold.* Don preferred working displays and stocking shelves over scalding his hands under the torchlike steamer for people who shouldn't be drinking the nasty dirtwater in the first place. The stuff wasn't even good for you. Don used to like coffee, but after working at Starbucks for a few months, he grew sick of it pretty quickly.

As he poured a bag of *Fijian Foglifter* into a saffron-colored glass container, he thought he heard someone walk up behind him. Before he could turn, Don felt a sharp, stinging *snap* against his right ear.

"Ow!" he screamed as he quickly turned around with his right arm up in the air for protection.

"Gotcha!"

With a devious look on his face, Brock Page came at Don again, flicking his forefinger at Don's other ear. Don deflected Brock's assault by grabbing his hand and turning it into a firm handshake.

"Dude, what's going on? I haven't seen you forever!"

"Yeah, it's been at least a couple months. So what have you been up to, Don?"

"Same ol', same ol'. Just stacking an expensive rack of go-go juice and doing school part-time. Nothin's changed. What about you?"

"Not much. Jay and I spent a few days 'boarding the Palisades awhile ago. *That* was intense. Then I went out to Joshua Tree for a couple weeks. I'm thinking about heading out there again this weekend. Wanna go climbing?"

"No can do. I've gotta work *all* weekend long. My roommate just bailed on me, and I'm stuck with the whole month's rent until I get someone to move in."

"Bummer."

"Tell me about it. Hey, I see your sister in here every so often. She's pretty cool, but I can't understand why she's going to school."

"Gina's like that. She's always been the A-student, Miss Motivated type of personality."

A slender girl wearing a green apron walked up to Don and asked him to cover for her at the espresso machine for a few minutes. Brock drifted over to the service counter while Don steamed a couple of vanilla lattes. As they kept talking, the bell on the front door jingled and in walked Max Henry looking for a late afternoon fix. Max frequented Starbucks, his favorite coffeehouse, especially toward the end of the week when his sermon prep went late into the afternoon.

Max strode to the register and ordered a double espresso with no foam. As he waited for his coffee, Max couldn't help but overhear the conversation of the two young men in front of him. He thought he heard Gina Page's name mentioned.

"Excuse me," Max interrupted. "I'm sorry to butt in, but are you Gina's brother, Brock?"

"Yeah, that's me," Brock replied in a wary tone to the stranger in front of him.

"How you doing? My name's Max. I'm a friend of Gina's, and she's always talking about you and your wild adventures. I hear you're quite a skier."

"Snowboarder," Brock corrected him with a wry look. "How do you know Gina?"

"She attends the church where I work. I'm the pastor over at First Church."

Don shouted over the whirling, sucking sound of the steamer, "You're a pastor? You don't look like one."

Max laughed and said, "No, and I hope I never do. I try to go incognito whenever possible."

Brock grinned and relaxed a bit. This guy seemed okay.

"Hey," Don said as he cranked the nozzle off. "Was that you who came in on the Harley?"

"Yeah, that's mine," Max replied.

"Cool bike. Man, I'd give anything to have one of those. I could hear that thing coming all the way down the street." Don handed Max the espresso.

"It's a lot of fun, but you'd be surprised how much work it takes to keep it clean."

"I can imagine," Brock offered. "Look how much chrome's on it. Can I ask how much you paid for it?"

Max lifted an empty hand and said, "Nothing; it was a birthday gift."

Don and Brock raised their eyebrows and met each other's eyes with a dumbfounded look. *"Not bad,"* they echoed.

"Do you guys ride?"

Brock shook his head as Don's eyes lit up. "I *love* to ride. My dad and I used to go out to Twenty-Nine Palms and race all over the desert, but that was a few years ago. I haven't ridden in a long time."

"Well, I've got to get going now, but next time I stop in, let me know when you're off work, and I'll let you take it for a spin."

"Really? Are you serious, man?" Don exclaimed.

"Yeah, why not," Max replied. "It's only a bike. I haven't had a chance to ride it much lately anyway. I'll see you guys later." Before Max left, he pulled a dollar out of his wallet and handed it to Don.

"What's this for?" Don asked.

"For making a good cup of mud."

"Cool," Don said. "See ya later."

As Max left out the back door to the parking lot, both Don and Brock commented how the First Church pastor didn't seem like a stereotypical church guy.

Thursday morning before work, Valerie Winslow sat at the yellow Formica table in her small kitchen in the Colorado Ridge Condominiums doing her nails and drinking a cup of coffee. She yelled toward Rikki's room and told her to hurry up for school or else they'd both be late. Valerie usually dropped Rikki off at school on her way to Coldman Real Estate Corporation, where she worked as an executive assistant to the president.

Rikki shouted back that she was hurrying, and, in a moment, she stormed into the kitchen, threw her books on the counter, and grabbed a bowl of cereal for breakfast.

"Now, honey, I talked with Dean again the other day, and he says the contract and the concert schedule are almost firmed up," Valerie said in between blowing her nails and applying a second layer of glossy red polish. "We should have the contract to sign by next week . . . isn't that fantastic?"

Rikki dreaded this moment. For the past few weeks, her stomach churned and tightened every time she wondered what to say to her mom about signing the contract. She and Gina Page had spent long hours discussing what they wanted to do with their lives in living out the promise they had made to God. As glamorous and exciting as a singing career was, Rikki knew it just wasn't right for her. She didn't want to spend the whole summer boxed up in a recording studio only to hop in a claustrophobic bus and spend the fall crisscrossing the country for concerts and eating fast food along the way. She didn't care how much money she got. It just wasn't important to her.

"Mom, I don't know how to say this to you, so I'll just say it; I don't want to do the record or the concert series."

"That's nice, dear. Finish up your cereal; we've got to get going." Valerie put the lid on the nail polish container, waved her hands, and drank a final sip of coffee.

"Mom! I just said that I don't want to do the record. Didn't you hear me?"

"Oh, I heard you all right," Valerie responded in a sharp voice. "What you *want* to do and what you're *going* to do are two different things. You said the same thing about singing for weddings and the Rotary Club. This contract is different; you know it is different. You can't always make decisions about your future based on what you want or feel like. I have worked far too long on this contract to have you sit down and tell me over a bowl of cereal that you don't want to do the deal. Is that understood?"

"Mom, I've thought and prayed a lot about this for the past couple of months. I don't mean to hurt your feelings, but my heart isn't in this project. I don't want to sing professionally now or in the future. It's not a question of what I want to *do* or don't want to *do*. I don't want to *be* a recording artist. For all the time that's spent in the recording studio, I feel like I could put it to better use serving others in a more practical way."

"What do you mean by that?" Valerie fumed. "Your singing *is* about God. It inspires other people to love him. Don't tell me you're taking that promise you made so seriously that you think you have to abandon your singing?"

"I'm not abandoning it, Mom. I just said I don't want to do the record. What I really want to do is work with Gina

Page and lead a kids' music program this summer at a soup kitchen in MacArthur Park. She's planning on buying the whole building and renovating it. I'd rather use my talents there."

"Kids' music program? MacArthur Park? Do you know what kind of people are down there?" Valerie gasped as she continued to wave her hands in the air. "Do you hear what you're saying? All this work for nothing? This contract is the only thing that can get us out of this terrible place," Valerie waved her hand around the kitchen while her head shook with rage. Mascara-soaked tears angled down her face, the small streams cutting through her blush-covered cheeks. "Don't you care about us? Don't you care about me?"

Now Rikki felt bad. Guilt stuck to her like a handful of wet, slimy mud. She swallowed and tried to ease the tension by saying in a soft voice, "It's not terrible here, Mom. You've done okay for yourself. We've always had enough. I'm happy."

"Enough! It's never been enough! Ever since your father left, we've never had enough! You've never seen the bills or the unpaid balances on my credit cards. *It's never been enough!* Can't you think of someone else's happiness but your own?"

Rikki had never heard her mom scream at her like that. She didn't know what to say next. In a rush of tears, Valerie grabbed a box of tissues and ran into the bathroom down the hallway. Rikki looked at her soggy cereal. She'd lost her appetite and didn't feel like going to school.

A few minutes later, her mom returned to the kitchen. Her makeup removed and still visibly shaken, Valerie gathered her things, headed toward the front door, and said to Rikki in a controlled, firm voice, "I'm late for work, so you'll have to call one of your friends for a ride to school. I don't want to hear any more of this nonsense about you backing out of this contract. While you're living under this roof, you'll do as I say." With that, Valerie left without saying good-bye and slammed the door on her way out.

At the Page mansion, Brock had just finished watching David Letterman in the game room when he heard screams coming from upstairs. Dashing up the long staircase two steps at a time, he tore into Gina's room where she lay huddled in bed with her eyes clenched tight, the sheets curled up to her neck. A long, keening howl came from her mouth, the awful cry seeming to emanate from the depths of what sounded to be a tormented soul.

"Gina! Gina! Wake up! It's me, Brock! It's only a dream!" Brock gently stirred her. Gina's screams transmogrified into a low, guttural moan as Brock pleaded with her. "Gina, wake up! It's okay; I'm here. It's just a bad dream."

Slowly, the moans faded. Gina emerged out of her disturbed sleep like a drowning person who'd just broken free from being trapped under an icy pond. Only moments earlier, her nightmare of weightlessly falling, falling, falling, flames, dismembered bodies, jet fuel filling the plane cabin, thundering crashes, snapshots of her mother and father, gentle snowflakes, and screams, endless horrific screams, had held her prisoner in a cold, unsympathetic terror.

"Brock?"

"Yeah, it's me. It's okay now . . . you're awake." Brock took his hand and wiped warm beads of sweat off her forehead. A tender smile of concern filled his face. "Same dream?"

Gina sat up in bed and said in a groggy voice, "Call it variations on a theme. Basically, yes."

"Always happens this time of year, doesn't it?"

A sullen look came over Gina's face. "Without fail. How come I'm the one who has the bad dreams and never you?"

"The sweet and innocent make a better target. That's why I always keep moving. You gonna be okay now?"

"Yeah, I'll be fine. Thanks, Brock."

As Brock left her bedroom and headed down the hallway to his own room, Gina got out of bed and went to get a drink of water. When she got back in bed, she couldn't go to sleep.

March 12. In one week was the anniversary of her parents' deaths. Ever since her parents' jet crashed into that Colorado mountainside when she was eight years old, Gina had been plagued by gruesome nightmares in the days surrounding the anniversary of the crash. Such markers weren't uncommon for grieving people, and as time wore on, the pain usually ebbed away. But for Gina, the haunting memories had lasted for years, returning each year out of the shadows as real, vibrant, and terrifying as the tragedy itself.

Gina grabbed the picture of her parents off the nightstand next to her bed and held it close to her chest. It was her parents' wedding picture. As Gina stared longingly at it, she began to think about the day when she would at last be united with them in heaven.

The little girl in her couldn't wait to run into her daddy's arms. One of the few memories Gina had of her father was when she used to run out the back door of the house to greet him when he got home from work. She could still smell the cologne on his collar.

Both her parents had been members of First Church and, as many of their adult friends had told her, each had had a sincere devotion to the Lord. Gina was grateful for this, and it was this hope that inspired her to use the money God had given her for his purposes and glory.

Ever since she made the promise in January to be Christ's disciple at any cost, it was precisely the question of cost that kept coming back to her. Gina had a net worth of over twenty million dollars. This sum, unknown to anyone but Aunt Florence, Brock, and a few close friends, provided her with every luxury possible for a pampered and carefree existence. But the idea of being set for life did not sit well with Gina, because that idea of life was largely defined by a materialistic and narcissistic American culture whose appetites were driven by greed, arrogance, and a complete disdain for God. Though Gina practiced discretion and modesty with her money, she was determined not to allow the seductive chains of wealth to wrap themselves around her heart.

As she lay in bed, she couldn't get the images of poverty and hopelessness she'd seen in MacArthur Park out of her mind. A week after reading about the closing of the soup kitchen, Gina had called Max Henry and Emilio Alvarez. Emilio gave her and Max a tour of MacArthur Park, explaining the drug and crime problems. Gina remarked how she had no idea how bad things were so close to her home. She'd seen homeless people in Pasadena and she knew San Marino had an Asian gang problem, but her life seemed so far removed from such social ills. What MacArthur Park really needed, Emilio said, was not just a soup kitchen to keep people's bellies filled but a mission designed to minister to the needs of the whole person. Food was a logical place to start, he noted, but think what could happen if a person's heart was also filled with the Spirit of God.

Ever since that little field trip, Gina had been seriously asking herself what Jesus would do. What was her life all about? What purpose did she ultimately have if she didn't use all that money sitting in the bank to benefit and improve the lives of others? What would happen to her wealth if she were to die tomorrow? Did her wealth mean anything if she didn't have love? Was her life just about gratifying her own wants and desires? Could she turn a blind eye to the needs of the poor and oppressed, the homeless and the hungry, when she had received from God more than she could ever need, want, or imagine?

Gina lay awake that night for hours thinking and praying about the burgeoning plan to fund a new mission enterprise in MacArthur Park that she felt God was directing her to put into action. She asked for wisdom and strength to make choices that would produce more than good intentions. She didn't want to stand in shame before Jesus someday and hear the words, "For I was hungry and you gave me nothing to eat, I was thirsty and you gave me nothing to drink, I was a stranger and you never invited me in."

Gina desperately wanted to keep her promise. It was like a hunger pain knawing inside her starving soul.

From the crypt of a terrible nightmare to dreams of seeing "the least of these" fed, filled, clothed, sheltered, visited, and loved, Gina eventually nodded off in tranquil sleep.

7

In the spring, it wasn't just the pink cherry blossoms at the Pacific Asia Museum, or the breathtaking fragrances in the Huntington Library rose garden, or the verdant green slopes of the San Gabriel Mountains that displayed the wonders of new life throughout Pasadena. Nature was but one reflection through the multifaceted prism of God's creative power at work. As never before in its history, First Church flourished with a passion for God and an authentic thirst for discovering true meaning and significance.

Max Henry's proposition back in January was initially met with skepticism and murmuring by the majority of First Church members. Now, in a strange and awesome display of God's movement through his people, over two hundred members of First Church had since pledged themselves to always asking themselves the elementary question of *What would Jesus do?*

Exciting changes took place as the elders, deacons, and members of First Church began to look at the unavoidable conflicts and complexities of life from a searching, personal perspective of Christ. Theological rhetoric and personal idiosyncrasies about how a certain program should or should not be run were overshadowed by a compelling urgency to love and serve others. Assumptions stemming from myopic statements like, "We've never done it that way before" or "We tried that; it'll never work" were challenged in a spirit of understanding and cooperation. The changes that came to the people and programs of First Church were not the result of emotion-driven, knee-jerk, change for change's sake decisions. No, every new idea was born of prayer, quiet reflection, and careful consideration of the steps and thoughts and heart of Jesus.

Every Sunday morning after the main service, the meetings in the fellowship hall were a time of sharing and laughing, praying and supporting, encouraging and enjoying the work of God's Spirit in each person's life. Hardly a week went by without someone telling a story of a significant risk he or she took for Christ that was contrasted by another story filled with tears, personal failure, and defeat. Everyone in the fellowship hall knew that asking what Jesus would do was a dangerous question of faith. Some people who'd attended First Church for years began to understand, for the first time, that failure was part of the process of following. For these people, the grace of God took on a whole new meaning.

Whether in victory or defeat, a key part of the meeting for almost everyone was the personal testimonies of the individual dilemmas, questions, and conflicts of the previous week. Each week the fellowship hall resounded with remarkable stories of faith and obedience. All springing from a single promise.

Ethel Parker, an elderly widow and longtime member of First Church, shared the story of reading in the newspaper about an African-American single mom with three kids who'd been swindled out of her home in a mortgage scam. At the bottom of the article, Ethel explained, was a number to call for those interested in offering assistance. Later that day, Ethel met the woman at her work and brought the whole family to live in her four-bedroom home until the mom was able to get on her feet again.

Scott Matthews told about a lunchtime Bible study he'd started at Pasadena High School with Rikki Winslow, Alex Powers, and a number of other kids in the youth group. The purpose of the Bible study was first, to grow in their understanding of God's Word. Second, every student in the group agreed to make friends with the loners and social outcasts on campus. Their goal was to be a friend to the friendless as Jesus would, especially at a high school campus known for its cliques and social exclusivity.

Gina Page shared about the remarkable cooperation that was taking place among Emilio Alvarez's church, First Church, and a few other small churches regarding the MacArthur Mission. Over the past two months, Gina had quietly established a foundation, bought the closed-down MacArthur Park Soup Kitchen building, and hired a construction crew to work on its major structural problems. Now the renovation was almost complete for the renamed mission, and an all-church workday had been planned for the following week. Also in the works was a summer school program for neighborhood kids and their families. The churches coordinated a drug and alcohol abuse program for adults to be held in the evenings. Staffed by pastors and trained counselors volunteering their time, the program would offer free baby-sitting and job training for individuals who wanted to rid their lives of chemical dependency. Volunteers were needed though, to run the youth programs that included athletic events, field trips to the beach and mountains, a music and dance program, vacation Bible school, and a summer camp at Big Bear Mountain the end of August.

Throughout the fellowship hall, various individuals stood up and told stories of being reconciled to relatives they hadn't seen in years. For many, all it took was picking up the phone and swallowing their pride. A few people shared how they had discovered newfound strength to control their tongue and temper at work. One woman remarked about the intimacy she found in spending time alone with God through prayer and reading Scripture. Two teenage guys stood and explained how they stopped dumping all their money into violent video games. Instead, they started sending money every month to a Christian relief organization that feeds and clothes poor children in Bolivia and throughout the world.

Last of all, Rikki Winslow stood up and told the crowd about the struggle she was having with her mom over the recording contract. After two months of volatile arguments, her mom had finally given her the ultimatum to sign the contract or find her own place to live when she graduated in June. Gina had already offered her a room at her house, but Rikki felt terrible that the conflict had gone this far. Still, she knew that God would take care of her regardless of what happened next. What she was most excited about in all of this was leading the music and dance program for kids at the mission this summer. Nothing could be more thrilling to her than teaching kids to sing and dance for the Lord.

When the meeting ended, Alex Powers hung around and asked if he could speak to Max in private. Max led him to his office where Alex sat down in a comfortable chair. Max asked him what was on his mind.

Alex had never sat in Max's office before and nervously crossed his legs as he wondered where to start. Only seventeen years old, he had made major technology presentations with ease and confidence to corporate marketing teams and executive boards about the intricacies of Internet cabling, bandwidth protocols, asynchronous timing mechanisms, and fiber optic switching equipment. Talking about personal matters was a different story.

Alex gave a slight cough and said, "I've been meaning for some time to talk to you about a difficult decision I'm facing. It's actually somewhat embarrassing to talk about, but I knew I could confide in you." Alex shifted in his seat and looked Max in the eye.

"Yes, Alex, what is it?" Max asked with a look of concern.

"PowerNet, the company I've been working at for the past year, just made me an offer to work for them as a full-time employee when I graduate from high school in June. I recently helped them design new software that enables banks to process account information quicker than the existing technologies in place. They're pretty excited about it. This last week, the company president took me to lunch at the Ritz Carlton, bought me a fancy meal, and made me an offer he said would make others drool. Once I signed the papers, he told me that I'd be able to eat at the Ritz any time I want. He explained that PowerNet is going public in a month and his offer wouldn't be on the table for long. He wants my decision in two weeks."

Alex looked perplexed and hesitant. With an opportunity like that for a young person straight out of high school, much less for anyone, Max wasn't sure why Alex wasn't going through the roof. Maybe at least his parents were.

"It sounds like you've got an incredible opportunity in front of you. The company even has your name on it! I think you've known for a while that for someone with your talents and capabilities, college seems like an afterthought, so what's wrong with the offer?"

"Nothing; it's a great offer. I'm guaranteed fifty thousand to start along with annual performance bonuses, but the real sweeteners in the deal are the stock options."

"Options?" Max's ears perked up. For the past few years he'd followed the amazing initial public offerings of California's most spectacular high-tech firms. Max had read article after article of tiny firms with two or three employees who'd become multi-millionaires overnight after inventing a new Internet search engine or writing a software program in six weeks.

Among the larger technology companies, the competition was fierce to hire the youngest, smartest, and most creative high school and college students. Offering no-frills base salaries to start, the compensation packages were then loaded with stock options that created paper millionaires at the moment of signing. Never before had an industry created such vast amounts of wealth in such a short amount of time. And here was young Alex Powers, a mathematical, computing genius and protégé of Cal Tech's finest professors, debating a decision that would be obvious to others.

"What type of options are we talking about, Alex?"

Alex arched his eyebrows and said, "To start, I'd receive fifty thousand shares at five dollars a pop. I'd then have fifty thousand more shares ranging in price from six to ten dollars a share in ten-thousand share increments. The stock's supposed to open on NASDAQ somewhere around eighteen dollars a share." Alex watched Max exhale a deep breath. "Pretty nice, huh? The president told me to consider it back pay for the bank software."

Max made a quick, rough calculation in his head. Almost two million dollars on paper. "The moment that stock goes public, you're going to be a very wealthy young man . . . and that's not counting if the stock jumps higher on opening day."

"Yeah, but that's not the real problem. What I'm wrestling with is the part of my job responsibilities that requires me to do certain things that I know for sure Jesus wouldn't do."

"What do you mean, Alex? I thought you designed software and gave presentations to companies explaining how it works."

"That's just part of what I do. I also spend a number of hours each week in the Internet commerce division of PowerNet. It's my job to check the redundancy software on the computer servers that host private company web sites. The redundancy software is a backup system that ensures a 24/7 link to the Internet in the event of a power outage. The problem is that the majority of these companies are adult web sites filled with pornographic material. PowerNet's known mainly for its software, but this division is one of their dirty little secrets they don't talk a lot about. I've seen a little of what's on those servers and some of it is pretty sick stuff."

"Yeah, and addictive too. I've talked with a lot of guys who're never tempted to buy pornography at a liquor store or walk into a strip joint, but once they get online, anything they want to feast their eyes on is literally one or two clicks away in the privacy of their own home. What are you thinking about doing?"

"Well, I talked to the president about those responsibilities and my beliefs and how I didn't want to be responsible for such immoral material. He didn't have a problem with that and told me he wanted me to focus on software development anyway, which is their core business. But I've really been wondering—what would Jesus do in my situation? Would he work for a company that degrades men and women made in his image? Would he even work in another division when he knew there were kids online from all over the world looking at obscene videos and pictures made available by his company?

"On the other hand, I've also thought that I could do a whole lot of good with a few million dollars. I could work for PowerNet for a couple years, watch the stock skyrocket, and when the time is right, sell all my shares. Then I could start my own company and help Christian organizations, churches, and non-profits in a way that could really make a difference."

"And prostitute yourself in the process, Alex."

"Yeah, that thought came across my mind too."

Alex didn't have to make his decision for another two weeks and hadn't yet told his folks about the dilemma he was facing. Max suggested he talk it over with them and get their input. Without telling him whether to take the job or not, Max counseled Alex to listen for the voice of the Holy Spirit and to guard himself against the love of money. Max read aloud the story of Jesus' temptation in the wilderness and closed their time together by praying for God to give Alex wisdom and discernment. In a strong, loving voice, Max encouraged Alex by saying he was confident that he would make the right decision.

Like almost every other business day for the past thirty-eight years, Sam Baker arrived at the Crankshaft Cafe on Monday morning at six o'clock sharp with the newspaper under his arm. The cafe sat on a corner opposite his truck-yard near the flower district in downtown Los Angeles and served as a general meeting place for all the drivers in Sam's company.

Sam moved toward his usual seat at the counter and exchanged greetings with Earl, the owner, who was busy frying an order of scrambled eggs and hash. From behind the grill, an old radio blared the day's traffic and smog reports. A crisp, salty smell of bacon floated through the air as Barbara, Sam's favorite waitress, said hi and poured him a fresh cup of coffee.

After dipping half a teaspoon of sugar in his black coffee, Sam opened the day's edition of the *Wall Street Journal* and scanned the headlines. Coca-Cola was up another two and a half points. That was good; Coke was one of the first stocks he'd ever invested in years ago and he'd held onto it through every stock split since. Didn't drink the stuff, though. Too sweet.

When his eyes came across the next article, Sam gasped and almost spilled hot coffee on his legs. He jumped out of his chair and asked Earl if he could borrow his phone. Earl said sure as Sam threw the paper on the counter and picked up the dingy white receiver.

Millennium Fund Manager Resigns
amidst SEC Investigation

Paul Wickman, one of the most successful mutual fund managers on Wall Street, resigned last Tuesday after members of his staff were convicted of insider trading. At the onset of the investigation, Mr. Wickman agreed to cooperate with investigators by testifying against the staff members named by the SEC. For the past six months, Millennium has been the target of an investigation stemming from large trades in the personal accounts of six Millennium staff members. Because of media attention stemming from Millennium's spectacular growth in recent years, SEC investigators began monitoring trades immediately before and after large position swings in the Millennium portfolio. Through a complex scheme of options trading, the staff members individually profited hundreds of thousands of dollars through shorting positions of popular science and technology companies.

Though not a target of the investigation, Wickman was said to be shaken by revelations of insider trading from members of his own staff. Citing ethical and religious reasons for leaving his post, Wickman stated, "For several months now, I have been seriously rethinking my investing philosophy concerning companies which I find morally objectionable, and I am sickened by the outrageous display of greed and arrogance demonstrated by select members of my staff. I have reached the point where I can no longer separate my personal belief in God and the actions required in my professional life. With this recent scandal, the violation of our shareholders' trust, and my personal values of integrity and honesty, I can no longer serve Millennium shareholders in good conscience."

When Max rang the doorbell at Paul Wickman's home after receiving Sam Baker's phone call, nobody answered the front door. He peered in a side window and didn't see any lights on or other visible signs of anyone in the house. Max walked around to the backyard, which was filled with large oak trees and an expansive, manicured lawn. The sprinklers were on, making a soft, fluid whispering sound throughout the grounds. He walked down a flagstone path, which was tinted a deep rust color from the sprinkler runoff. On the back porch, Paul Wickman sat motionless in a white Adirondack chair wearing dark glasses, a marine blue sweatshirt, wrinkled khaki pants, and a morose expression on his face.

Max pulled a chair next to him, and the two sat quietly for a few minutes.

In a low, catatonic voice, Paul spoke first. "Max, the past few days have been pure agony. Resigning from Millennium was one thing, the right thing. But Roberta taking the kids and leaving for her folks' . . ." Paul stopped, his voice cracking. Tears sneaked out from behind his sunglasses. "That knocked me sideways. I didn't think it would come to this."

Max sat knee to knee with Paul as Paul explained the events that led to his decision to cooperate with the SEC investigation and testify against his coworkers. When he had told Roberta of his plans to resign from Millennium, she had said that was the most outrageous thing she'd ever heard. He hadn't done anything wrong, so why resign? He had one of the most visible, prominent jobs in the mutual fund industry and a reputation to uphold here in Pasadena, she contended. What about her? What would all of her friends at the Annandale Country Club say? What about her role as chairperson of the Pasadena Arts Council? Had she spent years involving herself in countless charity events, civic programs, and social clubs just to see her influence and reputation washed away like a mudslide? And all because of a promise he had made to himself at First Church?

Paul went on to further detail how the tension had been rising in his marriage the past few months. Roberta claimed it was due to his religious fanaticism, but he'd never tried to persuade or force her to attend the meetings in the fellowship hall. She'd simply grown angry that he was taking his promise so seriously and accused him of being judgmental. This was confusing to Paul because he'd actually gotten better about being on time, attending social events that were important to her, and showing up at the kids' soccer games like she'd been begging him to. Before, he was very selective with his time, and his role as the fund manager always gave him an excuse to back out of Roberta's charity events and balls because he had too much work to do.

The SEC investigation was another matter. Paul couldn't just sit there and do nothing. He described feeling livid and betrayed by people who had used his leadership for their own selfish financial gain. He said the board of directors told him the alleged perpetrators would be prosecuted to the full extent of the law and, therefore, they refused to accept his letter of resignation. The board made all sorts of concessions and pleas. He was young and had an incredible future in front of him. There was nothing to be benefited by resigning from his role at Millennium. Paul would be given full authority to hire, fire, and retool his entire staff in order to rebuild his division with character, honesty, and integrity.

"It's like catching a falling knife. I no longer believed in a number of the companies we were investing in, and then the scandal imploded our division. Everyone was afraid. No one in the office was willing to step forward and speak the truth. I just didn't realize my decision would slice my family in half."

Max didn't know what to say. That was probably better for Paul, because if this would have happened six months ago, Max would have jumped in with all sorts of patronizing comments about conflict in marriage and quoted Bible verses as if they were capable of surgically excising emotional pain.

Max could tell by the vacant look on Paul's face and the lethargy in his spirit that the promise was taking its toll with devastating consequences and unfathomable pain. At this point, there were no words that could heal Paul's pain. Being present, together with Paul in his sorrow, was enough. Max put his hand on Paul's shoulder and silently prayed for his friend. He then got up, opened the patio door, and went inside to call Kate to let her know Paul would be joining them for dinner.

Kate put down the phone and asked Candice if she'd like another cup of tea. Wearing a pair of green overalls and an off-white, short-sleeved turtleneck, Candice patted her tummy and said the doctor told her to limit her caffeine intake for the baby's sake.

Sitting back down at the couch where she and Candice had been having their weekly Bible study, Kate said, "That was Max. He's bringing Paul Wickman over for dinner. He said Paul resigned from Millennium and, evidently, it's caused some problems."

"Well, if Max is being the friend to Paul that you have been to me the past few months, I'm sure he'll make it through whatever's going wrong." Candice leaned forward in her chair and set her teacup on the coffee table in front of them. "Kate, I don't know how to ever thank you for the support you've been to me. When I first found out I was pregnant, I thought I was going to die. I was so scared and so lonely. I didn't know who to tell or turn to. I don't know what I would have done without you."

Kate smiled, her cheeks lightly blushed. "Oh, Candice, you keep thanking me, but I haven't done anything more than any decent human being would. Let's just both thank God for giving you the grace to make such a difficult decision. How could I not help such a special person like you? When we're blinded by fear, we need each other to point out the God we can't see."

"I've never been so afraid in my life," Candice agreed. "Before I found out I was pregnant, never in a million years would I have considered having an abortion. But when I couldn't wash that little red circle off the pregnancy test, I wanted to kill myself. I was so terrified, angry at Jeff, angry at myself for being so stupid, afraid of what my parents would say, of what everyone at church and in the sorority would say. I've never felt so paralyzed in my life. Knowing what I know now, I'm so glad I decided to keep the baby. Still, I know this is only the beginning, and it's only going to get harder from here."

"That could be," Kate mused. "But just because you're having a baby doesn't mean you're destined for hardship and suffering the rest of your life. You made a couple of bad choices, and now you're determined to make good choices. That's what's so precious about God's grace—he can turn our mistakes and our sins into something beautiful."

It had been two months since Kate had received a phone call late one Monday night from Candice. She was in tears and apologized for calling at such a bad hour, but she really needed to talk. Kate asked her where she was, and Candice told her she was at her parents' home in town, but she didn't feel comfortable talking there. That gave Kate the signal she needed. She told Candice to meet her at the Denny's restaurant off South Arroyo Parkway in twenty minutes.

Kate arrived at the restaurant first, and when Candice entered they both went to a quiet booth in the back. There,

Candice broke down in tears and told her what a blood test had confirmed only days earlier. Over a couple cups of coffee, Candice related the whole story of her relationship with her former boyfriend and how he had almost persuaded her to get an abortion.

Jeff brushed the whole thing off as a mistake and told her not to worry about it. She had her future to consider, he said, and did she really want to spend the next few years changing diapers and waking up in the middle of the night to comfort a fussy baby. He didn't even ask her about her feelings or what she thought they might do together to deal with *their* dilemma. Jeff never referred to the baby as a human being. He always called the baby an "it." Then, she explained how he tried to apologize for going out with that other girl and how he made his best effort to patch things up between them.

That comment incited a fight, and Jeff stormed out to his car, but not before blaming Candice for being so unforgiving. Later, he called and apologized for screaming at her. He offered to take Candice down to the clinic where he would pay for the abortion and wait for her while the procedure was being performed.

Candice almost said yes, but she wanted another day to think it over. That night, she had a dream about Jack Manning's little girl, Ashley. In the dream, Candice saw Ashley wandering around a foggy cemetery holding a small bunch of white daisies, crying out for her dead parents. Candice called out to Ashley, telling her everything was going to be okay, that she was there to take her home, but Ashley couldn't hear her. As Ashley wandered farther away, Candice screamed louder and louder. Eventually, Ashley walked off into the fog, never returning, only the sound of her tender, searching voice echoing off the dampened gravestones.

Candice looked at Kate and told her how she had awakened in tears, crying for Ashley and for the baby inside of her. In her bed that night, she prayed to God, asking for the will and strength and resolve to keep the baby. In an instant—Candice snapped her fingers—the Spirit of God impressed on her heart the story of Mary and the virgin birth. Mary, Candice knew, could have been stoned for being found pregnant and unmarried in her day. Of course Mary hadn't been with a man as Candice had, but this Bible story of faith and courage gave Candice what she needed, even in the midst of her fears, to cement her decision.

That dream and the example of the young couple who faced ridicule and shame two thousand years before had prompted Candice to call Kate. Now, months later, Candice was living at her parents' home with a renewed commitment to the promise she made to God and a newfound friend in Kate Henry . . . and a baby due in the fall.

8

When twenty-five or so men, women, and teenagers from First Church arrived on Saturday morning at nine o'clock to clean and paint the MacArthur Mission, it wasn't the dog waste on the unmowed lawn, or the peeling ivory paint on the front door, or the trash along the sidewalk that bothered Gina. Nor was it the horrendous smell coming from the women's bathroom, though that was disgusting. The black, porous mold in the men's shower didn't look like it was too difficult to remove, but, thankfully, Gina didn't have to work in there. Gina, along with Alex Powers, Vic Gennaro, and three people from Emilio Alvarez's church had been assigned by Emilio to clean the kitchen. The kitchen, Gina thought, would be a cinch. No one had cooked in there for months, ever since the kitchen had closed its doors back in February.

Gina and the rest of her kitchen crew entered the darkened kitchen through a set of scratched walnut doors. The red floor tile was in suitable condition, not overtly filthy. A long, stainless steel food preparation counter stood in front of a box-shaped refrigerator with four doors. In the back were restaurant-style dishwashing equipment and stacks of amber-tinted plastic cups. A large mixing machine stood next to a stove that had ten burners, two ovens, and a wide grill. On white shelves adjacent to the refrigerator rested multiple stacks of rose-colored plates, utensil containers, unopened bottles of ketchup and mustard, and a long rack of cookware.

Armed with bottles of spray cleaner, sponges, brooms, mops, and rags, Gina's crew opened the dust-smeared windows and the kitchen's back door to let in some fresh air and zealously got to work. As Vic and Gina lifted a large trash can, a rustling, scratchy sound came from underneath it. To Gina's horror, a dozen or so thick, brown cockroaches scampered across her shoes. Gina unleashed a piercing, blood-curdling scream as she jumped onto the seat of a nearby folding chair. Vic and the others howled in laughter and initiated a brutal campaign against the gruesome invertebrates.

By noon, the entire mission had been wiped, swiped, scrubbed, swept, and mopped. Pastor Max and Sam Baker arrived soon after in Sam's truck, which was loaded with cans of paint, rollers, brushes, lumber, power tools, nails, and most important of all, ten large pizzas and a cooler of soft drinks for lunch.

As everyone gathered around three sets of tables in the cafeteria, Emilio blessed the food and thanked God for providing the people and the money to reopen the mission. Dressed in grubby jeans, T-shirts, shorts, old tennis shoes, sweatshirts, and an assortment of baseball caps and bandannas, the famished ministry team dug into the pizza like wolves around a kill.

Around the tables, people laughed and told stories about who had done the dirtiest deeds in each crew. Vic Gennaro grabbed a stack of paper plates and in bold red ink created a series of awards for various team members most deserving of admiration and honor. "Most Likely to Never Own a Dog," "Most Valuable Potty Scrubber," "Mr. Macho Moldy Man," and "La Princesa Cucaracha," were a few of the coveted awards given.

After lunch, Emilio stood up and introduced an older man named Slade Aguilar. Leather-skinned with kind blue eyes, Slade was a drug and alcohol counselor whom the MacArthur Mission Foundation had chosen as its new director.

Himself a recovering addict, Slade told the small audience how the Lord had freed him from drugs and alcohol ten years before after losing his job and being kicked out on the street by his landlord. Homeless, with a wife and two small children, Slade was desperate and turned to the Lord for help. It was in a small mission like this in downtown San Diego, Slade said, where he surrendered his life to God. After going through rehab and later repaying his debts, Slade began a new life of helping other addicts and homeless people get off the street.

The volunteers listened attentively, and when Slade was finished, they vigorously applauded. The joy and enthusiasm among the tables was contagious as people saw in Slade a glimpse of the healing and hope that could change the shattered lives soon to enter the mission doors.

After lunch, the paint supplies and lumber were brought in from Sam's truck, and the afternoon work session began. Max led one team painting the men's and women's dormitories in a soothing blue. Sam and three high school guys tore out the rotted stage at the far end of the cafeteria and refurbished it with new sheets of plywood. Jessica Matthews, her daughter, Kelly, and a few of her junior high friends painted funny cartoon figures in the children's bathroom, while in front of the mission, a group of college students trimmed hedges, mowed the lawn, and planted rows of fragrant gardenias along the entryway path.

By the end of the long day, everyone was exhausted but filled with an overriding sense of accomplishment. Max and Emilio gathered everyone in front of the newly renovated mission for a group picture. As the camera shutter blinked, over two dozen tired, dirty, and paint-spattered faces glimmered a radiant collage of joyful smiles and spontaneous laughter. A perfect close to a new beginning.

In the days that followed the mission renovation, Sam Baker spoke at length with Vic Gennaro about the changes Vic had made at his factory. Like Vic, Sam was getting on in years and, for the past few months, he had spent many hours deep in thought over the legacy he would leave with his company and his church. Though his trucking company had prospered, bringing him more material wealth than he could ever want or need, Sam lived a simple life. He was just as happy playing a game of checkers with the guys over at the cafe or working on his old Ford pickup as he was working to continue his company's domination of the trucking industry.

Sam's wife, Norma, had died three years before, just two weeks after their fortieth wedding anniversary. As difficult as that period was, Sam was glad Norma was in the Lord's hands. For years she had suffered with arthritis and had talked so much about someday being at peace with her body and at home with her Lord. Norma spent years in a wheelchair leaning on her God with an amazing faith that transcended the pain. Sam still arrived at work bright and early in the morning like he always did when Norma was alive, but now that he was alone in the evenings, he stayed at the office later than usual.

On Tuesday, organizing his desk at the end of the day, Sam pressed the button on the telephone intercom and asked his secretary to send in Max's friend when he arrived. A few minutes later, there was a light knock on Sam's door and in walked Don Marsh. Sam greeted him with a firm, calloused grip and asked the young man to sit down.

"So, tell me, son, Max says you're pretty good with your hands."

Don nodded his head and said, "Yes, sir, I like to work on cars and engines, but I've had no formal training or degree. Max and I stripped his Harley down a couple months ago and rebuilt part of his engine."

Sam chuckled. "That's what I hear. Max is a good pastor, but he don't know much about fixing things, now does he? He's what you call . . . how do you say . . . mechanically challenged."

Don laughed and leaned forward in his chair. "Yes, sir, that's why he called me. After he let me ride his bike, I told him I heard a noise in the engine. He said he'd take care of it, and three hours later I got a call from him asking me to come over and help. When I arrived at his house, he had that bike spread all over the driveway like it'd been run over by a truck."

"Ol' Max, he'd better stick to preaching and taking care of people before he gets himself into more trouble. Tell me son, what do you know about trucks . . . I mean big rigs, semis?"

"Well, as I mentioned, I've never had any formal schooling. No, I've never worked on big rigs before."

"Formal schooling? Who's talking about degrees and diplomas? See these hands here?" Sam held out his wrinkled, callus-covered palms. On the tops of his hands, nicks, scars, and white, old tissue marbled over blue, sinewy veins. "This here's Mr. Iron, and this here's Mr. Steel. They've been all the education I've needed to build this company. These are my diplomas. I don't want to hear what you don't have. I want to hear what you can do and if you're willing to work hard."

Don perked up in his chair. Max and Gina had told him a lot about Sam, and now he could see why they liked him so much. There was a spark of life in the old guy's words. Don liked that. All his life, he'd constantly been told what he couldn't do, or what a poor student he was, or how lazy he was, or how he should show a little more initiative around the house. He remembered very few moments of happiness growing up, at least while his parents were still together. After his dad left his mom, she spent all of her time thinking about herself, going out at all hours on week nights, and hardly ever being home on the weekends. Don spent most nights in high school home alone watching MTV and eating cereal for dinner.

"See this picture here of my drivers? Some of these men have been with me over twenty-five years. A few of them started out younger than you. To each one I said, 'If you're willing to work hard, treat our customers right, and be honest, I promise to do my best to see that you have a job for life and a healthy retirement fund to show for it.'" Sam folded his hands and leaned forward on his desk. "Tell me, son, how do you like where you're working now?"

Don looked down at his lap and mumbled, "I hate it, sir."

"Now, why's that?"

"Because there's no future in it. I can't see myself making coffee for the rest of my life. It's like most of the jobs I've had out of high school. All of them have been to just pay the bills, but I can't see them leading me anywhere. All of my friends are either away at school or traveling around the world or at least doing something they like. They have their parents to pay for everything, but I'm on my own. I don't want to make any excuses or expect any handouts, but this life is definitely not a level playing field."

"No, life isn't fair," Sam agreed, "and those people who think it should be or that the world owes them something are the most miserable people on earth. Life is what the good Lord allows you to make it, and that is what it becomes." Sam stood up and walked around his desk. "Come on, son, I want to show you around the yard and have you meet some people."

Sam and Don left his office, walked through a series of hallways, and finally entered an enormous warehouse filled with hydraulic forklifts, stacks of wooden crates and shipping pallets, men holding clipboards and walkie-talkies, and work crews loading semi-trucks that had backed into one of the forty bays.

The warehouse was noisy. Red safety lights flashed on the forklifts and sirens bleeped whenever someone was backing up. The idling truck engines rumbled and pounded in unison like a thousand stampeding horses. Men shouted orders and commands over the din as if they were military commanders preparing for an overseas operation.

As Sam and Don walked along the cement walkway, people nodded and waved to Sam in friendly deference and went back to their work immediately. Don observed that the workers were focused, industrious. He didn't see people who looked like they'd lounge around or cut corners when the boss or manager wasn't looking. That was a far cry from the workers at the previous places he'd worked. Himself included.

After a good hour of touring the warehouse and truckyard, pulling back the cab on a couple of semis, and looking at the difference between Peterbilt and Mack engines, Sam walked Don to his car and asked him what he thought of the whole operation. Don told him it looked interesting and commented what a great thing it must be to drive all over the whole country and get paid for it.

"Tell you what, son," Sam started. "I could tell within two minutes that you're the type that needs to be outside doing something with your hands. You got about as much business being in school as you do trying to be a pumpkin. I can't give you a diploma, but I can give you a job. Teach you how to drive a truck. Let you see some of this great country. Eventually, you'll make enough money to raise your own family and never worry about putting bread on the table. Ask any of my men; they're loyal to me 'cause I'm loyal to them."

"That sounds great. Uh, I mean, are you sure?" Don asked with excitement rising in his voice, yet wondering if the old man's offer was too good to be true. It wouldn't be the first time Don might be disappointed by broken promises. "You don't even know me, Mr. Baker."

"No, I don't, but I learned a long time ago that if I was ever going to grow this business, I needed to be willing to take some risks. I'd be silly to stop now . . . and don't call me Mr. Baker. Everyone around here calls me Sam."

"Yes, sir, I mean . . . Sam."

"When can I expect to see you in here? When can you start?"

"Well, I have to give my notice at work, but I work in the evenings for the next couple weeks anyway. If I can be out of here by four, I can start next Monday morning."

"Good," Sam said as he began to roll down his shirt-sleeves from the cool of the approaching twilight. "Be at the Crankshaft Cafe—it's right over there on the corner—at six o'clock sharp on Monday morning. I'll introduce you to a bunch of the guys, and we'll go over some of the things you'll begin to work on first around here. In a few months, we'll have you licensed and ready to drive one of those rigs. How's that sound?"

"That sounds great!"

"Six o'clock Monday morning."

"Yes, sir, Sam," Don said in a voice bursting with vibrance and energy. He felt like someone had just pulled a thick, black cloak from his head, and for the first time in God knows how long, that this life, *his life,* had opportunity and promise.

Sam smiled with a look of gentle compassion and shook Don's hand with a firm grip. He could see the change in the boy's eyes, a different person than the one who'd entered his office an hour earlier.

The two said their good-byes. As Sam strode back toward the building, he turned around and said, "Oh, and Don, one more thing . . ."

Oh, no, Don thought as a sharp whip of tension cracked at his spine. One more condition, he feared. One more thing to make this whole deal impossible. *It's gonna cost me money. Or, there's no job. He's just playing with me. Another broken promise, only this one's really sick and twisted.* Don forced a hesitant smile and weakly said, "Yeah, what is it?"

"It's what I tell all my truckers." Sam grinned. "Don't be late."

It had been a week since Alex had talked with Max Henry and his parents. When he explained to his mom and dad about PowerNet's offer, they were so happy they laughed and hugged him like never before: Their son was going to be a millionaire! But when Alex explained about the other part of his job, maintaining the computer servers filled with pornography, his mom was taken back a bit. Under a brow of seriousness and concern, Alex could tell his dad was chuckling inside.

Alex's parents never did do a very good job with "the talk" about sex and all that. Now, Alex was awkwardly trying to explain his ambivalence and aversion about working for a company that promoted such a malevolent distortion of God's creation.

"Now don't start sounding like a religious fanatic here," his father asserted in a stern voice. "We're talking about your future, Alex. What people do online is their business. You can't be responsible for other people's decisions, immoral or not."

"I'm not trying to be responsible for other people's decisions," Alex countered. "I'm trying to be responsible for *my* decisions, and I don't think Jesus would work for a company that exploits women and children."

"Would you *puhleeez* . . ." his dad moaned.

"Alex, listen dear," his mother cut in. "You are a very talented and intelligent young man. Your father and I know that your youth group and church work are important to you, but there comes a time when you have to start thinking about yourself and your future. God doesn't expect you to save the whole world, you know."

"Mom," Alex implored, "I'm not trying to save the whole world. I'm just trying to do what's right."

"Alex," his father butted back in, "I don't think you fully understand what this opportunity is all about; we're talking about millions of dollars here. Don't be foolish about your ethics and morals. Work for PowerNet for a few years, and you'll never have to work another day in your life."

Like Rikki's conflict with her mom about the recording contract and Gina's argument with her aunt over her intention to keep the promise she had made at First Church, the debate in Alex's home on whether or not he should take the job with PowerNet also erupted into a fight. Both sides pleaded reason and moral certitude. Neither side was willing to give ground in the name of family, money, allegiance, or duty.

One question.

A simple promise.

Could there be a loyalty that proved stronger than the bond of blood?

A week after the fight with his parents, while at his workstation ripping out the wiry innards of a server that had a fried motherboard, Alex overheard the snickers and muffled laughs of two young coworkers as they clicked through screen after screen of obscene pictures and video clips. He had one week left to give the president his answer, and anger surged in his veins. *This just wasn't right!*

"Hey, Alex," one of the guys named Tim called from behind the monitor. "Come check this out! I've got a date here for you on Friday night, but I'm not sure if it's a 'he' or a 'she'!" When Alex told them he was plenty busy, the two laughed hysterically and poked fun at what they called "Alex's sexual repression."

Out of their view, Alex stood at his computer workstation, closed his eyes, and prayed.

In a moment, his decision was made. PowerNet could keep their two million dollars.

9

ello, Mrs. Ritter. My name is David Matthews, and I'm calling from the Security Insurance Company. You recently filled out one of our response cards, and I'd like to tell you . . ."

Click!

It was seven-thirty in the evening. David was tired of sitting at his desk for so long, tired of rejection. He took off his telephone headset, stretched his arms above his head, and then picked up the silver-framed picture on his desk. It was a photo of Jessica and the kids in an aluminum fishing boat taken during their summer vacation to Mammoth Lakes two years before. Scott and Kelly were both holding the rainbow trout they'd caught. Jessica had a beautiful smile on her face, as white and radiant as the spring snow remaining on the surrounding peaks.

David sighed. There would be no summer vacation this year. Meeting his family's financial obligations was still a month-to-month battle, an ongoing struggle that had no end in sight for at least the next couple years. David wondered if this was what all guys go through when they switch into a totally new career they are unfamiliar with.

Year-to-year renewal policies was where the long-term money was made, and David still had a long way to go. The only money he was making right now was a small base salary, which was a draw against commission. For every hundred cold calls he made, eight to ten resulted in personal appointments. Out of those came one or two, maybe three closes. His referral business was picking up, but it was still sporadic at best.

Months ago, he had cut back from working five evenings a week to two. That was the biggest step of faith David had taken in a long time, but surprisingly, the Lord had provided just enough to make it through each month. He had been able to make Scott's basketball games on Tuesday and Friday nights as well as have a date night with Jessica every Thursday. As a result, things had definitely improved around home. Scott was honoring his promise to be home before curfew, and he was more involved in the youth ministry than he'd ever been. David's time with Kelly was precious, and her hugs when he arrived home made him feel like the richest man in the world. Ever since he and Jessica had promised to ask what Jesus would do, their marriage had been marked with a new sensitivity to one another's needs and feelings. It was as if they had broken through a solid granite wall in their level of understanding and communicating with each other. He and Jessica had been enjoying a profound level of intimacy they hadn't experienced in years.

"Hellooo . . ." a soft voice sounded from outside his office door. "Anybody in there?"

"Come on in, Kim. Nobody here except us phone lists."

Kim Carlson sauntered into David's office like she occasionally did whenever he worked late. Dressed in a tight-fitting, black skirt and a pink blouse the shade of cactus flowers, Kim walked over to the chair in front of David's desk and sat down.

"So how goes the war tonight? Any good leads?"

David laughed. "Good leads? Those are about as hard to find as gold in the L.A. River. I feel like I'm ice fishing on a very cold and lonely lake."

Kim raised an eyebrow. "Oh, yeah? Well, maybe you need something to warm you up. Why don't we blow outta here for awhile and go get a drink? You're hardly in here in the evenings anymore."

When David began working at First Security last year, he went out a few times for dinner with the other salespeople. They usually went to the happy hour at the El Torito on East Foothill at five. After an hour or so of downing ninety-nine-cent beers and munching on chips and guacamole, the office gang trooped back to the office to make another round of calls until eight or so. But bars never really appealed to David. The only reason he went was for the camaraderie and a chance to get to know his coworkers better.

Tonight, the office was uncommonly quiet. As usual, Kim was working late. She was a veritable phone animal, one of the top producers in the office. At twenty-eight, she was single, confident, and ferociously attractive. Five-foot-ten with a slender, athletic build, she was the type that caused traffic accidents when walking across the street. With wavy, shoulder-length, blond hair, engaging blue eyes, and a riveting smile, she could be simultaneously playful and coy. On the phone, depending on the prospect, her voice was as sultry as smoke, or if she had a woman on the line, she was all business, as if she owned First Security herself. Her words either soothed as a light caress or were sharp, rational, and convincing. Kim sought mostly appointments with men, with whom she had a 75 percent close rate. It wasn't uncommon for her to get a phone call a few days later from a client wanting to take her out for the evening. Kim always said no. She was calculating and discreet. Rarely did she mix business with pleasure.

"The food at El Torito doesn't do much for my waistline."

"Oh, David, you're in great shape," Kim flattered. "Most of the guys around here let their bodies go years ago. You're the only one worth looking at anymore," she teased. "Come on; pull yourself out of that chair, and let's go get a drink. We can be back to work in half an hour." Kim moistened her lips, her smile seeming to drip like golden honey.

"Come on, Dave," she plied innocently.

David paused for a moment and took a long breath. Maybe just for half an hour, he reasoned. What could be the harm? He had told Jessica he'd be home no later than nine. He'd always had a professional relationship with Kim. There was no reason to think that tonight would be any different.

"I don't know," David said, rubbing his neck and stretching his arms above his head. "I've got a lot of work to do. I was thinking about making a few more calls and then leaving for the night."

Kim frowned. A second later, she sprang out of her chair with a look of concern on her face.

"Is your neck sore?" she asked, walking around his desk and behind his chair. "Here, let me rub it for you. My neck gets like this all the time."

Before David could object, her strong, warm hands were on the base of his neck massaging his tense muscles in a rhythmic, kneading motion. Her summery touch was intoxicating. Like a wild goose shot out of the sky, David dropped his neck and moaned in relief.

This feels so good, David thought. *Only a couple minutes.*

"There," Kim whispered. "I knew you'd like this. These magic fingers don't even cost a quarter."

As Kim's hands identified and rubbed the tight knots in his shoulders and neck, David became more aware of her tranquilizing, spell-like presence. The sweet wafting of perfume. The tender clip of long fingernails scratching the hair above his neck.

What transpired next happened faster than a lightning strike across a blackened, cloudy sky. Kim spun David's chair around, and before he could raise his eyes, she was moving toward him with all the fiery passion of a blazing Pacific sunset.

"Whoa!" David cried as he grabbed Kim's shoulders, stopping her lips inches from his face. Over his shoulder, he could see his wife and kids smiling at him from the fishing boat picture on his desk. "Kim, we . . . we can't do this!"

"Oh, Dave," she said breathlessly, trying to nestle her face into his neck. "You can't be serious. There's no one here but us."

Dave tried to stand up, but Kim forced his arms down in the chair.

"Kim . . . no! I'm serious!" David said emphatically. The back rub was one thing, but this had gotten out of control. He knew he had to get up and leave quickly. He could tell by the look in Kim's eyes that this woman was on a mission.

At six-foot-four, David was considerably stronger than Kim. In a sudden move, he grabbed her shoulders tightly and stood up, the strength of his grip eliciting a small cry from her lips.

"This has gone far enough," he rasped in anger for allowing himself to be sucked into this briary web of lust and deceit.

"Why don't you go on home to your wife and kids," Kim fumed as she knocked the silver-framed picture off the desk and stormed out of the office.

Recognizing the rich heritage and beauty of their town, the locals of Pasadena were often fond of saying, "When you decide to make Southern California home, you may as well move to Pasadena right away. Because sooner or later you will... or wish you had." With its stately, opulent mansions, trendy shops, corporate headquarters, restored Craftsman and California bungalow homes, world-renowned research centers, charming neighborhoods filled with oak- and sycamore-lined streets, the home of the annual Prime-Time Emmy Awards, and a population of just under a hundred forty thousand people, Pasadena had been characterized as the world's smallest major city.

But for all the wonders and marvels of living in a semi-arid city with an average annual daytime temperature of seventy-six degrees, Pasadena was just a microcosm of the greater Los Angeles area. Los Angeles, the City of Angels, had its own demons. A colder side. A darker personality. A lurid underbelly of crime, misery, squalor, hopelessness, and urban blight. The poor neighborhoods and substandard housing of downtown Los Angeles shared nothing in common with the environs of the wealthy northern and eastern suburbs.

MacArthur Park was a festering sore in the middle of Los Angeles, an infected area of squalor and corruption where homeless people wandered the trash-strewn streets pushing all of their worldly possessions in a single shopping cart. It was a lost world caught in the blurring haze of crack fumes and crystal meth; a sanguinous battlefield that consumed innocent victims in driveby shootings; a place of alcohol abuse and addiction; a war zone of rival gangs and staccato gunfire at all hours of the night. For those who struggled to raise their families in safety and responsibility, free from the lure of gangs and the venom of drugs, it was a brutal and coarse life. It was here that the MacArthur

Mission once again opened its doors like a blazing lighthouse beacon in the tumult of the urban storm.

The cooperative ministry of First Church, Iglesia de Fe, and several other Hispanic and African-American churches officially began the third week of June. Max Henry, Emilio Alvarez, Michael Lloyd of the African Faith Center, June Higgins of the United Methodist Church, and volunteers from each church comprised the ministry leadership board that oversaw the mission's operations in the community.

Since late April, Rikki Winslow had worked extensively with Emilio Alvarez and several other volunteers to recruit workers for the summer mission kids' program. So far, she and her team had recruited over a hundred and fifty volunteers who were responsible for vacation Bible school, arts and crafts activities, soup kitchen responsibilities, reading, math, and computer lessons, baby-sitting in the evenings, summer camp athletic events, field trips to the L.A. Zoo and the Getty Center, and the upcoming summer camp in August. At first, the task seemed overwhelming. Rikki's team had hit the phones hard calling every family at First Church, making presentations at all the churches involved and at her school Bible study. They even contacted all the First Church high school graduates away at college and asked them to spend their summer as day camp counselors, teachers, coaches, program leaders—anything to be involved in the lives of children and families in MacArthur Park. Two weeks before school got out in June, several teams of students and adults fanned out in the neighborhoods surrounding the mission. Knocking on doors, the teams introduced themselves and explained the summer children's program that was beginning at the mission in late June. Many families were excited to see the schedule of outings and events available at no cost to their children. Two families even asked if they could help out a few days a week. Soon, everyone in the neighborhood was talking about the

MacArthur Mission and the changes taking place there. The cumulative effect of the multi-church effort of prayer, hard work, and undoubtedly God's blessing, united a team of eager workers poised to do what Jesus would have done in the portion of Los Angeles many churchgoers preferred to overlook.

On a Saturday night in late June, the MacArthur Mission held a grand opening fiesta celebration. In classic Southwest style, a huge feast of Mexican specialties filled the long tables in the colorfully decorated cafeteria. From throughout the neighborhood, families streamed into the mission for the free meal and a chance to see the new children's center with the playground in back. Word had gotten out on the street that the kitchen was reopening, and dozens of homeless people showed up looking for a hot meal, a warm shower, and a safe, comfortable place to sleep.

In one corner of the cafeteria, a trio of mariachis played lively, festive tunes while a dozen or so kids improvised their own creative dance moves that brought smiles and laughter to everyone. Everyone who'd accepted Max's challenge on that Sunday morning at First Church six months ago was busy at work: Paul Wickman and David Matthews served enchiladas and rice in the food line; Jessica Matthews, Kate Henry, and Candice Sterling were helping homeless moms and their children get checked into the women's dormitory; on the new playground, Rikki Winslow, Alex Powers, Scott Matthews, and a bunch of other high school students kept the forty or so screaming kids somewhat in control; Gina Page prepared food in the kitchen with her brother, Brock, and Don Marsh, who she enlisted after much haranguing and the promise of a free meal; Vic Gennaro and Sam Baker walked around the crowded tables with pitchers filled with Coke and juices, asking people if they'd like a refill. A couple of times during dinner, Emilio Alvarez made the announcement that there would be special music and a short message immediately following the meal.

Throughout the rest of the mission, dozens of other volunteers worked tirelessly, a contagious enthusiasm shining on their faces. People greeted visitors at the door. Fresh towels and clean-smelling soap were handed out in the shower area. Guided tours were given to the neighborhood families and members of the churches involved in the mission effort. Dirty dishes were washed. Old, filthy clothes were replaced with neatly pressed seconds. Sign-ups were taken for vacation Bible school, summer school, field trips, and summer camp. Flyers and brochures for the drug and alcohol, parenting, and career development workshops were distributed to the adults. In all, the eagerness of Christians serving a neglected and forgotten neighborhood in the name of Christ initiated the tearing down of walls and the building of what could become a community of peace and reconciliation.

After dinner, Emilio stood before the crowded hall and introduced Slade Aguilar, who greeted the mission guests and explained the upcoming summer programs. When he was finished, he turned the microphone over to Rikki. Accompanied by an acoustic guitar player and a girl playing an electric keyboard, Rikki's beautiful, haunting voice drifted through the cafeteria like a slow fog coming in off the ocean. The crowd quieted and listened intently to Rikki's song of God's forgiveness and grace. The global collage of faces—Asian, Hispanic, African-American, and Caucasian—couldn't resist the magnetic pull of the melody and the irresistible charm of Rikki's humble demeanor. All were focused forward, any sneering remark or outburst immediately silenced. When the song ended, a vigorous round of applause thundered throughout the room.

When Rikki gave the mike to Pastor Max, the thundering didn't cease. Max thanked Rikki and announced who he was and what church he was from. At that, in the back, a mildly inebriated homeless man belched loudly, and the crowd roared with laughter.

Another homeless man from across the room stood and mocked, "The pastor of First Church? When I lived in Pasadena, I went by that church a dozen times, and I never received so much as a nickel from them!"

A large, ruddy-faced woman yelled, "Yeah, my landlord attends First Church, and you should see my rent bill. It's even going up next month!"

Several people stood and told the troublemakers to sit down. Others yelled back and told *them* to sit down, only these individuals used colorful adjectives and obscene gestures to get their point across. From all over the room, people cried, "Give the guy a chance!" "Get those losers outta here!" "We want Rikki! We want Rikki!"

Max began to panic. He'd never dealt with an unruly mob like this before. He was used to the quiet, respectful, well-mannered people of First Church who respected him as their pastor and friend. He tried to quiet the crowd, but the confusion and clamoring increased. He sensed a full-blown riot about to explode as the noise and yelling continued to escalate. He signaled to Emilio to do something . . . *anything* . . . to help him.

Emilio ran over to Rikki and the two musicians who were sitting in a corner with concerned looks on their faces. Emilio huddled and spoke to them for a few seconds. In calm fashion, the three strode back on stage. Rikki gave a 1-2 count and the two musicians ripped into a fast, energizing rhythm that silenced the clamor like a punch to the mouth.

Cheers and clapping replaced the screams and obscenities as a wave of cold sweat and relief broke out across

Max's face. He'd never seen anything like it. Before Rikki reached the chorus, like a lion tamer before a cageful of wild and angry beasts, she had hundreds of yelling people yielded and subdued. To think that Rikki could have been wrapped up in studio recordings and concert schedules right now instead of quelling this riotous mob—Max shuddered to imagine what could have happened without her presence here.

From the kitchen, Brock and Don laughed about the whole scene, claiming that if the police showed up in riot gear, they were out of there fast. Still, Rikki's song had the same effect on them as it did on the masses in the cafeteria. Brock stared at Rikki and wondered if she'd ever consider dating someone like him. Probably not, he surmised. He was far too independent and, as Gina had told him not a few times, way too cocky for someone as poised and sensible as Rikki.

Rikki's song ended. Max rose to the stage for another try. This time, though, he was calmer. During her song, Max had prayed and asked for peace. He asked God to give him the words, *the right words*, to share with the people of this neighborhood. Now, he began to look at the people before him with new eyes. What would Jesus do? What would Jesus say? Who were these people? Strip people of their material possessions, socioeconomic positions, and societal roles—yes, line everyone up in their bare humanity, and you had starving souls in need of God. And what was the message of Christ? Jesus came for sinners, not the righteous. He came to seek and save those who were lost and not those who had no need of repentance. And it was with this confidence that Max Henry spoke of the love of Jesus and his calling for all to follow in his steps.

Before, what did Max have in common with the poor and the homeless, the panhandlers and the prostitutes, the addicted and the insane? A dollar here and there given away on a street corner. His old clothes given away to the Salvation Army. Sure, he previously agreed with the leaders of other soup kitchens and shelters for battered women who came to his office seeking help that these were indeed serious social and spiritual issues, but like all ministers, he was busy. His church, like any other, had inner conflicts, building issues, weekly programs, warring committees, overworked staff members, and budget problems to resolve. Taking time to help other ministries and nonprofit organizations that weren't connected to the purposes of First Church had never captivated his attention or imagination. Anything outside of his church and the needs of his well-dressed people—like the mass of humanity in front of him now—was the work of other individuals and groups who had their own calling.

Tonight, though, Max couldn't ignore the appearance of need and desperation on individual faces in the crowd whose lives and backgrounds were so different than his own. He now honestly felt compassion and love for those he'd previously scorned. He had been praying the last few months for God to transform his narrow-minded and self-centered heart. So many sleepless nights he'd wondered what it would take to rid himself of his prejudices, his pretension, his contempt for those he considered pathetically lazy and weak. Now he couldn't help but imagine that Jesus probably felt the same fears, hopes, needs, and anxieties emanating from the multitudes as Max was now experiencing. More amazing than the stillness of the now-attentive crowd, Max was in awe of the God-given love he felt for every person in the room.

After the meeting was over, the cafeteria cleared, and the mission volunteers began cleaning the grand celebration mess. Slade and a few newly hired staff members oversaw the details of helping over two dozen of the mission's new guests settle into the men's and women's dormitories. An hour and a half later, Max and Emilio gathered the entire ministry team together in the cafeteria for a few minutes of thanking God for a wonderful (albeit hectic) evening and for the exciting summer ministry awaiting them.

The following Sunday morning after the service, the mood in the fellowship hall was electric. Everyone, it seemed, had something to share about what had taken place at the mission the night before. One man told how he and a friend walked around the park before the fiesta began and persuaded a number of homeless people to come in for a meal and a shower. Another recounted speaking to a homeless family—a man in his thirties, his wife, and their three kids, who arrived in the mission parking lot in their rusted Chrysler LeBaron, which they'd been living out of the past month. He introduced the man to Vic Gennaro and, after Vic spoke with him for about twenty minutes, hired him on the spot.

One woman stood and shared how she had the opportunity to share Christ with two prostitutes who said they wanted to leave their line of work but were in fear of their lives if they tried to do so. A couple of teenage girls told heartbreaking stories of talking with children on the playground who said their parents were so addicted to crack that the family food money often went for drugs. On and on, people of all ages in the fellowship hall stood and told their personal stories. Some were inspiring testimonies of what God was doing in people who'd surrendered their lives to him; others cast bleak portrayals of the utter despair of those who'd walked through the mission's doors, reminding everyone of the magnitude of the work yet to be done.

Not wanting to quell the overwhelming optimism pervading the room, Max still cautioned everyone that they were outsiders, uninvited guests in fact, to the people of

MacArthur Park. They had to earn the right to be heard, and the only way this could be done was through their actions first. The homeless, the needy, and the addicted of MacArthur Park needed to see the life of Jesus Christ through deeds of love and mercy. Max quoted the words of St. Francis of Assisi, "Go and preach the gospel. And if you must, use words."

When Max was finished, Rikki gave an update about her current housing situation.

"True to form," Rikki started, "the day after graduation two weeks ago, my mom kicked me out of the house just like she said she would. She told me she felt betrayed for my not signing the recording contract. She wished me a wonderful life and told me she never wanted to see me again." In tears, Rikki looked at Gina and choked, "I want to let all of you know, especially Gina, how much I've appreciated your prayers and support. This has been the most difficult decision I've ever had to make in my life, but after seeing the smiles on those children's faces last night and thinking about what amazing things could happen at the mission this summer, I know I made the right decision. Nothing will be more thrilling than seeing the kids we work with begin to ask what Jesus would do in their own lives."

Everyone in the room, now over two hundred people, broke into cheers and applause for Rikki. When the room quieted, Paul Wickman apologized for having to share this, but said he was dying inside. His wife had filed for divorce despite his pleas for reconciliation and, for once, to think of the kids before her reputation in the community. Citing irreconcilable differences due to his religious fanaticism, his wife threatened to sue him if he didn't agree to a fast and, in her words, "mutually beneficial" divorce. Paul asked for prayer that his marriage might be saved. He also asked the group to pray for his wife and especially the kids, who were wondering why Daddy never slept at home anymore.

In a humble voice, David Matthews stood next to his wife, her hand in his, and told about the close call he had had at work the previous week. Without going into explicit detail, he accepted full responsibility for not recognizing temptation and allowing himself to cross the line; he advised the other men in the room to reevaluate their boundaries and personal standards for their professional lives.

"I thought I was stronger than that," Dave explained. "Jessica and I have been growing closer and closer the past few months. But that's what's deceiving about temptation: It's when we think we're strongest that we're really the weakest.

"Understandably, this incident has sent a shock wave through our marriage. I've confessed my irresponsibility and my sin of lust to God and Jessica, and asked their forgiveness." Turning to Jessica, Dave said in a deep, heartfelt voice, "I just want to state publicly that I am reaffirming my vow to be faithful to you, Jessica, throughout the rest of our marriage."

A sobering silence hung over David's words. Throughout the room, everyone quietly acknowledged in their hearts that it was indeed pride that came before a fall. Whether that fall was lust, greed, idolatry, gossip, or murder in one's own heart, no one could judge the actions of another without first examining their own heart. David's words were a powerful reminder to everyone that the promise they made to God wasn't a magical shield from sin and temptation, nor did the promise guarantee an unfettered journey through earthly streets of gold in glorious Christian victory.

No, with the promise came a cost and with the many stories that had been shared, it was often costlier than ever imagined. It was a daily decision fraught with persistent questioning. Inner debates of the soul. The risks of ridicule and rejection by one's own family members. The loss of sure or promised wealth. The stark realization of one's true spiritual poverty realized in moments of weakness. A denial of self.

As many had discovered so far, the promise *was* painful. There was joy and peace and purpose and contentment, but there was also conflict and suffering and sorrow and pain. The promise hurt and would continue to hurt, at least for this life.

Max surveyed the somber faces across the fellowship hall. He knew the call of Christ and the cost of the promise were unpopular messages not only for the world but also for a diluted church culture that reeked of hypocrisy, judgment, materialism, and the avoidance of personal discomfort. It had always been so much easier to preach soft, inspiring messages that appealed to the masses. Max could now see his previous fears for what they were. It wasn't that his messages had lacked substance, but he sometimes felt that if he preached more strongly, he might offend some members or they might stop giving to the church. Before, Max never doubted his motives, but he knew better now. Who, but God himself, knew the hidden motives that had caused Max to hoard his comforts and possessions rather than risking all to build the kingdom of God?

Reflecting on the whirlwind of events of the past few weeks and months, Max now had a whole new understanding of the words of G. K. Chesterton: "Christianity has not so much been tried and found wanting, as it has been found difficult and left untried."

After Max closed the meeting, he thanked Dave for his honesty in front of so many people and encouraged those in need of prayer or counsel to stick around.

Standing before everyone in the crowded fellowship hall, Max offered these final words of encouragement: "Last night was a new beginning for the mission and what appears to be a great work of God. Let's remember to keep our eyes and hearts on him, not the work. If we continue to love God with our whole heart, soul, mind, and strength, the work will take care of itself as he works through you and me. And what a beautiful work it will be."

10

box of half-eaten chicken chow mein with noodles hanging over the edge sat on a stack of floppy disks on Alex Powers's cluttered desk. Three empty Coke cans stood next to the computer monitor as he banged away at his keyboard. Alex looked at the clock next to his bed. Three A.M. Like many programmers in the computer industry, Alex had little need for sleep when consumed with a gripping idea. It had come to him right before he decided to go to bed. That was just before midnight.

Now, as he held the computer mouse in his hand, ready to click the send button, he decided to read the email one more time, wanting to be sure he had left nothing out.

```
To: calvinb@earthnet.com
CC:
BCC:
Attachments:
Subject: Work of the Holy Spirit in Pasadena

Dear Calvin,
    I've been meaning to write you for over a
month now, but it seems that lately my every
```

waking moment has been spent at the MacArthur Mission, or on the baseball field with the neighborhood kids, or on field trips going to all sorts of places in L.A. with seventy-five screaming kids, or cleaning scummy dishes. I hope I don't sound like I'm complaining, because I'm not; I love the mission work we have going on in downtown L.A., but I can't believe it's already the beginning of August. I got this wild idea a couple hours ago and I need your help. But first, I need to get you up to speed about everything that's been happening at my church the past year.

I've told you before about my pastor, Max Henry, right? He's been here at First Church for nine years and from all appearances, he's set—a good salary, plenty of perks like golf at private country clubs, free Rose Bowl and Laker tickets. The guy even rides a Harley that the church gave him on his last birthday. First Church, over a hundred years old now, has always had a reputation for taking care of its pastors. As the oldest and wealthiest church in Pasadena, it's filled with a lot of old dough and some of the city's most respected families. I guess it's the kind of church where a lot of seminary grads would love to go and "suffer for the Kingdom."

Well, I had never liked Max much. The guy always had a cocky attitude, like he was God's gift to Pasadena. The adults at church have always liked his preaching because he's smart, good-looking, and sometimes funny. Most of my friends and I thought he was too flashy and dramatic. Fake too. Never got much out of his messages.

Anyway, last January, after this homeless guy bursts into church and knocks himself out (that's a whole other story . . . I'll email you later on that one), Max stands at the pulpit the next Sunday looking like death warmed over and asks everyone in the audience to not do anything for a whole year without first asking the question "What would Jesus do?" Regardless of the cost or sacrifice, each person was to do, in their best judgment, what Jesus would do.

That was the most radical thing I'd ever heard Max say, and I accepted his proposition. So far, the results have literally changed my life, but I'll tell you more about that later. Since that first Sunday, almost half of all First Church members have made this promise, and as word has spread about the remarkable changes taking place at First Church, there're now churches all over California that are doing the same. This promise, movement, work of the Spirit, whatever you want to call it, is spreading, and the results are incredible. I've heard countless stories of whole families and individuals making radical lifestyle changes and decisions. I couldn't possibly go over what's happened to everyone who made that promise here at First Church, but here are a few examples.

After first railing on Max, I must come to his defense: The guy is a different man. When he preaches now, his messages are simple, straight to the point, right from the Bible. Before, he'd quote Jean Paul Sartre, Madonna, Bill Gates, Homer Simpson, and Jesus all in one breath. He doesn't wear the expensive suits or flashy ties like he used to. Just normal pants and a cotton shirt like the rest of us humans. He used to wave his hands and arms from the pulpit like a hyperactive cheerleader, but now he speaks quieter and with a deep sense of conviction. You should have seen how pretentious he used to be, telling everyone about how he had dinner with Congressman such and such, or how he was invited to speak at Christian conventions all across the nation, or how First Church had grown 20 percent the past year due to his commitment to the community. So what, I often wondered; does that really impress God? But now, Max never talks about himself. The guy is so humble and loving and sincere you'd think that he'd been substituted with a long-lost identical twin. He is not the same man I knew eight months ago. Every Sunday morning when we meet in the fellowship hall after church, Max greets everyone by name, asks how we are doing, and always has something encouraging to say. Though he didn't want anyone to know about it, Max and his wife canceled their trip to Paris this summer and gave the money to a poor family. He's even worked with the elder board to free up funds for the mission project.

Remember the girl I told you about, the one whose parents died in the plane crash years ago? Well, for as much money as she has, you'd never know it. I've gotten to know her well the past year, and the question she's obsessed with is, "What would Jesus do with so much wealth?" That question could intimidate a lot of people, but she asks it with such authentic humility and an eager desire to do what's right that everyone can see she's seriously interested in their thoughts about the matter. After a lot of prayer and discussion with our pastor and the pastor of a local Spanish-speaking church, she established a foundation to help fund the renovation of the MacArthur Mission. The foundation also pays for staff members' salaries, camp scholarships, computers and supplies for the mission learning center, and the development of new programs for children and families. What's even more amazing than that is her brother became a Christian last week during one of the services at the mission. I don't have a lot of time to tell you about him, but let's just say he's traveled the world in search of the ultimate extreme experience. He said that after evaluating his sister's life and reading the Bible on his own for awhile, he could no longer ignore what he called, "the avalanche of God's love." He also said that all the snowboarding and rock climbing in the world couldn't compare to what he found in Jesus.

One family at First Church has been through some heavy problems the past few months. It's been no secret that their family's been struggling with finances ever since the father lost a high-paying job at some company in town. Last year, the teenage son had a growing reputation around campus as an up-and-coming partier. Even though he occasionally came to youth group and said all the right words, you could tell the guy was a total poser. He's a good basketball player, and evidently he was ticked off at his dad for never making his games, so he'd stay out drinking 'til two in the morning. When his folks accepted the pledge, things started to change around their house. He and his dad worked out their problems, and ever since then, he has been firmly committed to following God. He, another friend, and I lead a Bible study at our high school with about twenty other kids. We've even gone to other youth ministries to tell about how making this promise to God has changed our lives.

If you can believe this, the girl who sings solos at church walked away from a six-figure recording contract that her mom and agent had been working on for months. She was tired of all the demands being placed on her by her mom and, as they got closer and closer to landing the contract, felt that a recording career was not where the Lord was leading her. What she really loves is working with children. She'd much rather help poor kids with an after-school song and dance program than seek fame and fortune with her voice. Because of not signing the contract, her mom kicked her out of the house and she's now living with a friend. She has done an amazing job coordinating the volunteers for the whole summer program at the mission. She even prevented a near riot on the opening night of the mission by calming the crowd with a couple songs.

The former manager for one of the strongest mutual funds on Wall Street goes to First Church too. He recently resigned from his job because of insider trading going on among his own staff. He even agreed to help SEC investigators by testifying against the alleged insiders. What he really had trouble with though was the stocks that the fund was invested in. Ever since he made the promise to make his personal and professional decisions based on what Jesus would do, he could no longer agree with investing in companies that polluted rivers or exploited workers or made bombs. His decision has cost him big. His wife has filed for divorce and custody of their two kids. He's devastated, but despite all the hardship he's faced, he continues to remain faithful to the promise he made.

Ironically, a few weeks after he resigned, he received a phone call from the president of a company that makes land mine detection equipment. The company has developed a new chemical sensor unit that sniffs out molecules from underground explosives. The president heard about his resignation, read his comments about ethical responsibility in the Wall Street Journal, and asked him to interview for their CFO position. He was offered the job, and now he's playing a part in helping to eradicate land mines throughout the world. That's at least one positive development in all his turmoil.

There's a UCLA graduate who came to Christ at a campus Bible study meeting the night before Max made his challenge to First Church. A month or so later though, she discovered she was pregnant from a relationship she had bro-

ken off in early January. The guy wasn't much
help and tried to persuade her to have an
abortion, but she refused. She's fully committed to raising the child as best she can as a
single parent. She's living with her folks
here in Pasadena and has become good friends
with Max's wife. I'll let you know if she has
a boy or girl.

One of the friendliest persons at First
Church is a guy who owns the Leatherworks
chain, and from what I've heard, the changes
he's made at his factory have attracted the
attention of many other companies in the garment district in downtown L.A. He said that he
always kept his church life and business life
separate, but ever since he made this promise,
he began making changes in a competitive
industry branded for abusive sweatshops. He
first started with cosmetic changes, like
refurbishing the lunchroom area with new
paint, plants, vending machines, tables, and
chairs. Then he replaced the old, hardwood
chairs with soft, adjustable office chairs for
the older women who had to sit all day long at
their sewing machines. He initiated an
employee profit-sharing program based on annual
revenues and a monthly bonus program for each
work group. Every fourth Friday, Max and the
Spanish pastor come to the factory for a
lunchtime Bible study for those who want to
attend. If you ever get out here, you'll have
to meet him.

As for me, I know you've been wondering what
I decided about PowerNet's offer. I never
imagined that a hobby I started eight years
ago would lead to a lucrative contract filled
with tempting stock options. After a lot of
thought about the pornography issue and debating what I could or couldn't do with all that
money, I decided that God is more interested
in my obedience than my money. It's not that I
wouldn't like to be wealthy, but if I have to

sell my soul to get it, I'd rather work at Taco Bell. As Max said, I've got plenty of opportunities ahead of me. I might as well pick one where I can truly help others and honor God in the process.

Yes, there are some incredible things happening with me and at First Church here in Pasadena, and at the MacArthur Mission, but before you or anyone else who reads this email thinks that these changes have come without conflict or resistance from members of the church, I need to tell the other side of the story as well. Within the first month of the one-year promise, a number of families did leave the church. A few wrote scathing letters accusing Max of violating the sacred traditions of First Church. One lady even accused Max of starting some kind of new religious cult. You know how they say sacred cows make great steaks? Max has certainly had his share of bull.

For those who stayed at First Church but didn't make the promise, there were rumors that a few of them were going to try to force Max to resign. Fortunately, some of the most prominent people and many of the church elders are a part of this movement, and the work of the Holy Spirit has produced so many positive changes that there isn't much for these whiners to grumble about.

I have to admit that, at first, I had my own questions and doubts about all this. I wasn't alone in asking how far I was supposed to take this promise. Was I to become like St. Francis of Assisi? Was I supposed to give away my brand-new computer and walk around eating nothing but locusts and honey? A few friends and I peppered Max with all sorts of questions. He said that as far as he could see, Jesus' words do not produce a legalistic requirement for every person to abandon all earthly possessions in order to go live in a

cave. But if the Spirit impressed on an individual that something must be given up in
order to follow him, it was the responsibility
of that person to make the decision for or
against such a sacrifice. That's the beauty of
this promise: In the spirit of Christian freedom, it is between each individual and the
Spirit of God to ultimately figure out what
Jesus would do in this modern age. No one can
dictate the decisions of another.

As you can see from the stories I've told
you, there has been no lack of courage about
making personal sacrifices so far. These people
are just a handful of those here at First
Church who are earnest about discipleship and
what it means to call themselves Christian.
I'm afraid the name of Christ has been used
almost to the point of irrelevancy here in
America, and taking on a challenge like this
is one way (not the only way) to demonstrate
an authentic and practical love for God and
others. Maybe words mean so little precisely
because they're fleeting? Action, on the other
hand, can be measured, evaluated, and put to
the scrutiny of unbelieving hearts. I've written this email in the hope that you will act
on the following idea.

If you've been inspired or intrigued by our
story, I'd appreciate it if you'd forward this
email to everyone on your personal email list.
After that, I'd be grateful if you'd post it
on your web site and in the various newsgroups
in which you participate. Since we don't want
to spam anyone, please ask everyone who
receives it to forward it only to those people
on their lists that they know personally.

I finally developed this idea after talking
with Max about the possible effect of our experience on the church in general. We wanted to
let other churches know about how God's Spirit
has been working here at First Church and the
changes that have taken place in people's

lives, but we were wrestling with the best way to do it. The Internet may not be the most effective medium for sharing these stories, because there's nothing like hearing them in first person, but it sure is good at reaching a lot of people. At least this is a start, and it will give people from all over the world a chance to evaluate it for themselves.

As Max and I talked the other day, he said, "Suppose people in churches all across America made this promise and lived up to it! Do you know what a revolution that would cause in Christendom? Why not? Are disciples of Jesus supposed to do anything less than throw down their nets and give all to follow him? Is the test of discipleship any less today than it was in Jesus' time? If First Church could change its way of doing things, couldn't the whole church raise the standard for following Christ? I'm not talking about changing creeds or splitting theological hairs, but about what could happen if Christians just changed the way they think and act toward people who don't know Christ."

Well, Max and I began to dream about what could happen if churchgoers made this promise, not by force or obligation, but out of a pure and simple love for God. There's no telling what could happen if everyone would ask themselves this basic question. I hope you've been encouraged by these stories and that you will forward this email to your friends as soon as possible. I look forward to hearing from you soon. When you thaw out in Chicago, hop on a plane and fly out west to see me.

Sincerely yours,
Alex

11

"Okay, I want everyone to listen up!" Gina Page commanded through a squawking bullhorn. "You are to board the buses with your counselor according to your cabin assignments. Nobody can get on a bus if they're not with their whole cabin."

Three orange school buses were parked along the street near the front steps of the MacArthur Mission. Judging from an outsider's perspective, this late August, Saturday morning scene of over a hundred nervous and boisterous fourth, fifth, and sixth graders, most of whom had never been to the mountains before, as well as their parents giving kisses good-bye and trying to quiet their younger children who were crying because they didn't get to go, appeared to give new meaning to chaos theory.

A team of college- and high-school-age guys loaded duffel bags and sleeping bags onto the buses. Camp counselors yelled out the names of the kids in their cabins and asked them to sit in cabin groups on the lawn. A few last-minute sign-ups anxiously waited at a small folding table to be assigned to a cabin. Small groups of boys ran all over, oblivious to the calls of their parents, pinching and teasing girls a foot taller than themselves.

From all the nervous energy in the air, it seemed like some of the kids were ready to explode with excitement. All the enthusiasm, vigor, and overwhelming sense of adventure in the smiles in every child's face could have powered L.A. for an entire month. None of these kids had ever had a whole week of hiking, swimming, waterskiing and tubing, singing at night by the campfire, playing games, making crafts, shooting arrows, learning to rock climb, and breathing fresh, smog-free mountain air!

When the buses were loaded, a Toyota 4 X 4 screamed into the side parking lot. Out jumped two young men. They threw down the tailgate and unloaded their gear in a hurry.

"You're late, Brock!" Gina yelled through the bullhorn, just to rub it in, as her brother approached the school bus.

"I hit traffic when I went to pick up Don."

"Traffic? This is L.A.! A carjacking I would understand, but you get no slack for the traffic excuse." Gina laughed and gave Brock a hug. "Hi, Don."

"Hi, Gina. Where are our kids?"

"Over there on the lawn . . . in the hot sun . . . *waiting for you.*"

Don and Brock walked over to the group of black, white, and Hispanic kids and introduced themselves. Pulling out a family-size bag of chocolate chip cookies as a peace offering for being late, Brock doled out handfuls to each kid while other kids looking from the bus windows screamed, "Hey, that's not fair!" and "Over here, over here! Gimme some! *Pleeease!*"

Gina smirked. "You two show up late, buy your kids off, and then cause a near riot. Get on the bus before I crumble one of those things down your shirt."

"Got milk?" Don and Brock laughed in unison and ran up the bus steps, narrowly avoiding Gina's swing.

Vic Gennaro, Rikki Winslow, and Alex Powers walked up to Gina and saluted in mock deference to the camp director.

"All prisoners accounted for, sir, er, ma'am," Vic said in a quick military clip.

"Good job." Gina giggled. "Let's lock and load!"

"Aren't we forgetting something, Gina?" Rikki asked.

"Oh yeah, we'd better pray. We're going to need as much prayer as we can get."

With that, the four bowed their heads in the midst of well-wishing parents, shrieking kids on the bus, crying children, and two bearded homeless men who sat on the front steps and shook their heads in amazement, wondering out loud why any adult in their right mind would board those buses.

This week of camp, ending during the Labor Day holiday weekend, was the culmination of a long, hot summer filled with new friendships, pool parties, softball games, Bible lessons, field trips, encouragement, and tutoring support for kids who struggled in school during the year. Parents throughout the MacArthur Mission neighborhood had learned to trust and depend on the mission volunteers to take care of their kids while they worked. Not only did this save the parents a pile of money in child-care and baby-sitting expenses, it also won their hearts through the church services held every week in the mission cafeteria.

On Saturday nights, Rikki and a small band led worship, alternating between songs sung in Spanish and English. Max, Emilio, or one of the other local pastors preached the simple gospel message of Jesus coming for the sinners and the sick. Each week, whole families, runaway kids who were the victims of physical and sexual abuse, discouraged single parents, crack and crystal meth addicts, homeless people, battered prostitutes, and former gang members with tattoos all over their bodies, came and wept at the sound of Rikki's voice. This mottled mess of humanity, victims of neglect, poverty, and abuse, was inescapably drawn to the mission for the love and compassion they were so desperately seeking.

Depending on God for strength, as well as the support of the mission staff, many had enrolled in the midweek drug and alcohol recovery programs. Slade Aguilar worked tirelessly, often long hours into the night, developing new programs and training additional staff. Introductory Bible studies were held in the mornings and evenings to help new believers learn to walk in the steps of Christ. Through a newly formed neighborhood watch program and the increased support of local police, the crime and gang activity that had once plagued the park across the street dropped considerably. The mission soup kitchen had a magnetic pull on the hungry and homeless, who also found much-needed shelter and the respite of cool air-conditioning from the simmering August nights. Even a small church nearby, which had wanted to start a meal program for elderly shut-ins but didn't have the facilities, began to use the mission kitchen in its off hours.

The mission became a center of change and a lighthouse of opportunity for hundreds of broken lives who'd lived far too long in poverty and shame. The transformation had begun. Signs of visible growth and the pervasive work of the Spirit in people's lives were abundant. Many churches, *the Church* in this community, had awakened to serve "the least of these" mentioned by Jesus over two thousand years before. And almost every summer evening, the neighborhood kids returned to play on the playground as the glowing orange sun disappeared in the west, far from view atop the jungle gyms' highest bars.

12

ush, Candice! Push! You can do it!"

"*AAAIIIEEEEE,*" Candice screamed in agony, her body searing in pain like the blistering asphalt outside in the hot September sun. The air-conditioned maternity room provided little relief for her discomfort. Hot drops of sweat poured down her red, flushed face. "Kate, I can't push anymore. It hurts too much."

Kate stood back. A nurse wearing turquoise scrubs spooned ice chips into Candice's parched mouth.

"Okay, that's enough," Dr. Lucas said as she stepped forward with a serious look on her face. "Candice, we're going to have to do a C-section. The baby's getting distressed, and I don't want to take any chances. You've been at this for hours, and you've given it your best shot, but it's time to get that baby out of there." The doctor immediately picked up a phone and called the nurses' station to prep the operating room.

A few minutes later, Candice was wheeled into the labor and delivery operating room. Kate walked to the waiting room where Candice's parents, Bob and Annette Sterling, and her older brother, Jon, were anxiously wondering how Candice was doing.

"Candice just headed into surgery for an emergency C-section. She's been pushing for too long, and the doctor said the baby's heartbeat was slowing down too much. The doctor said it shouldn't be much longer and not to worry."

Annette Sterling held her hand to her mouth, longing to comfort Candice as if her daughter was a little girl again and had fallen and hurt herself on the playground.

"Why are they calling it an emergency C-section?" Bob Sterling asked casually, trying not to show the worry growing inside.

Jon stood there silent, not knowing what to say, eyebrows slanted in concern.

"It's an emergency because they weren't planning on delivering the baby that way. The doctor said this happens quite often with first-time mothers," Kate reassured Candice's parents. "You'll have your first grandchild in no time—thirty, forty minutes at the most, the doctor said. I'll give Max a call; why don't you have some coffee while you're waiting?"

After calling Max at the office and asking him to come to the hospital, Kate joined Candice's family in the corner of the waiting room where they drank coffee and made small talk.

An hour and a half later, the elevator doors on the maternity floor split open and Max sprinted down the hallway to the waiting room, where he found Kate outside the door, arms folded, and head hanging low.

"Hey there. What's wrong?"

Kate crumpled into his arms and cried, "The baby was doing fine at first, but after a few minutes, she stopped breathing. They had to resuscitate her, and now she's in the neo-natal ICU."

"Hmm," Max reflected. "What has the doctor said so far?"

"Nothing more than that. We haven't heard anything since they told us the baby was having problems. That was thirty minutes ago."

"How are Bob and Annette doing?"

"Bob's trying to be optimistic. Annette is a nervous wreck. Jon's in there too."

"Let's go in and see them," Max said as he put his arm around Kate, who leaned into his shoulder, and the two entered the waiting room.

As the two families hugged one another, few words were said. There really wasn't much to say. The only thing they could do was wait and pray. Max led the group in a short, quiet prayer, and the five sat for a long, torturous hour.

Finally, the waiting room door opened and in walked Dr. Lucas. Her smile of greeting relieved the worried family and friends.

"Congratulations, Mr. and Mrs. Sterling. You have a brand-new, yes, healthy, granddaughter. She gave us a good scare there for awhile, but she's going to be fine."

"Hooray!" the Sterlings and Henrys cried.

Tears of joy streamed down many faces as everyone in the room shared hugs, congratulations, and thanksgiving for answered prayer.

"When can we see Candice and the baby?" Mrs. Sterling eagerly asked, her proud voice resonating a privileged domain known only to grandmothers.

"You can see them right away," Dr. Lucas replied. "They're both resting in Room 4-B."

With that, the waiting room emptied, and the five dashed down the hallway, barely able to keep from breaking into a full sprint.

Max reached the door first and held the door open for the Sterlings, followed by Kate, who arrived last.

They found Candice sitting up in a bed near the window, her blond hair tied in a pretty pink bow. In the crook of her arm was a small bundle wrapped in a pink blanket. Candice looked up at her newly arrived visitors and broke into a tired smile that radiated calm and contentment.

Bob Sterling approached the bed and gently kissed his daughter on the forehead. His wife burst into tears at the sight of their new granddaughter asleep in Candice's arms. Jon smiled and greeted his sister, letting her know how worried everyone had been for her and the baby. Kate and Max stood in the back of the room next to a table and two chairs, not wanting to be too intrusive during this sacred family moment.

Breathing fast and steady, the baby's little red cheeks were like soft rose petals on a sweet summer day, her white fingernail tips long and delicate like tiny, translucent seashells. Around her small, well-proportioned head was an elastic pink bow, the same shade of pink as Mommy's. A silky crown of thin, golden-blond hair glowed in the slants of light waning through the tinted window. The baby yawned and opened wide, revealing U-shaped gums that glistened like saltwater rippling over a sandy shore back to sea. Her tender lips were precious crimson folds, awaiting a lifetime of kisses.

Annette Sterling motioned for Max and Kate to come and see the baby. Kate shuffled forward in excitement, the look on her face as if she'd just won the California Lottery. Max followed, and the two stood next to each other on the opposite side of the bed.

"Oh, Candice," Kate cried. "I'm so proud of you! Look at her; she's beautiful!"

Candice could hardly contain herself. "She's so sweet; I love her so much."

Max had a lump in his throat, and his eyes were watering. "Congratulations, Candice. Kate and I are so happy for you.

You're going to make a great mommy." Max stopped and tilted his head to one side, a quizzical look riveting his eyes. "I'm sorry, but I'm missing something here; what's her name?"

Overcome with emotion, Candice replied in a small voice, "Hope."

13

In the fall, throughout Pasadena, the golden autumn leaves quickly turned a deep burning scarlet and soon fell to the ground as the city braced itself for an unusually cold and wet winter. Thanksgiving passed, and the MacArthur Mission sent out its holiday meal teams for the second time in a month to the impoverished areas of Los Angeles.

At five-fifteen on Christmas Eve, the Matthews family pulled into the Happy Trails Trailer Park in Altadena looking for space number thirty-six. This was their last stop for delivering Christmas meals. The decrepit park was packed with fifty old, rusting trailers on a small, two-acre parcel of land near the base of the Angeles National Forest. Makeshift antennas and electrical lines criss-crossed the sky. Muddy puddles of water pooled in low spots across the crushed gravel parking lot and streets that were littered with dented and abandoned cars, old engine parts, corroded patio furniture, broken green glass, and a child's deflated ball. Beat-up washer and dryer units lay sideways on the ground. Soggy scraps of trash lay strewn throughout the grounds.

Down one of the park's narrow side streets, two little girls were sitting on a small, green Astroturf porch playing with dolls. David pulled his car alongside the trailer, and Jessica rolled down her window.

"Excuse me, girls, do you know where Bill Hutchenson lives?"

The two girls looked at each other and giggled shyly.

The bolder of the two spoke. *"No hablamos ingles."*

Jessica said, *"Gracias,"* and rolled the window back up from the biting chill of the early evening air.

From the backseat, Scott and Kelly waved as their father moved on.

"It has to be here somewhere," Jessica said, "but none of these spots are marked."

"This place is an absolute dump," Scott remarked. "It reminds me of the time we went to Tijuana for the day. I never knew we had this much poverty so close to home."

"Amazing to think a place like this is only fifteen minutes from home," David pondered. "Certainly puts our finances into perspective."

"There it is," Kelly blurted. "Right on the side of that trailer—number thirty-six!"

David stopped the car in front of a small yard that was surrounded by a waist-high chainlink fence. Tied to a metal stake on a short leash, a black pitbull dozed on a wet piece of brown shag carpet near the trailer's front door. The Matthews got out of the car and walked to the gate.

David held a foil-covered plate that was dripping gravy out the side and onto his right hand. Kelly carried a small plate of cookies wrapped in clear green cellophane with white snowflakes. Scott and his mom each had Christmas gifts in their hands for the elderly owner of the trailer.

"I'm not going in there," Scott complained. "Look at that dog! He'll eat all of us for Christmas dinner!"

"Oh, Scott," his father admonished, swinging the gate open. "Don't be so dramatic. The animal's asleep. It's not going to hurt anyone."

While David shut the gate and his back was turned, the *clink* of the gate awoke the dog. The dozing beast leaped to its feet baring sharp fangs, barking incessantly with rabid snarls. Its thick, muscular neck strained against the chain anchored in the ground.

Startled, David jumped like he'd stepped on a rattlesnake, almost dropping Bill Hutchenson's Christmas dinner on the muddy gravel. Jessica pulled Kelly close to her and stepped back toward the car.

Scott keeled over in laughter and reprimanded his father, "See, Dad! I told you so! The dog's a killer!"

From inside the trailer, a gruff voice yelled out, "Can't you keep your mouth shut, Elizabeth! Be quiet!"

Jessica looked at David, his cheeks flushed with fear, and said in a hushed whisper, "I didn't know he had a wife. It sounds like they're having an argument. Maybe we'd better come back tomorrow?"

Just then the trailer door opened and out walked a tall, heavyset man wearing a camouflage green bathrobe. The robe barely fit around his waist, exposing a large pair of baggy, grey boxer shorts. A thick rug of chest hair covered his upper body, and his oily, matted hair looked like it hadn't been washed in weeks. In his hand was a freshly popped, foamy can of beer.

The man looked at the snarling dog and growled, "Shut up, Elizabeth!"

Oh my, Jessica thought to herself before she said, "Mr. Hutchenson, my name is Jessica Matthews and this is my husband, David, and our two children, Kelly and Scott.

We're from the MacArthur Mission, and we've brought you a Christmas dinner and some gifts."

The man lumbered forward, reeling from the beer in his system.

"That's mighty nice of you folks," Bill Hutchenson wheezed as he stood on the other side of the fence and scratched the dark growth on his chubby jowls. "Don't mind old Elizabeth; she's a bit protective of me. We're all each other's got."

The five stood there for a few minutes, talking in the frigid night. Elizabeth had calmed down but still eyed David with vigilant suspicion. Bill apologized for not inviting them in, but he wasn't expecting company. The place was a mess, ya know.

When it didn't seem like there was much more to say, Bill made a couple trips back and forth to carry everything to the trailer and thanked them for coming. David and Jessica invited Bill to the Saturday night services at the mission and wished him a merry Christmas.

As Bill walked back to the front step of the trailer, the Matthews loaded into their car and waved good-bye. The car pulled away, its headlights navigating around the murky puddles, its four occupants quietly reflecting on how much they really had.

The other places they'd visited that night weren't as bad as this trailer park. Dave was grateful to have a decent paying job. It wasn't a lot, but compared to this, it was enough. Jessica wondered how lonely Bill Hutchenson would be on Christmas Day and said a silent prayer for him. Scott was happy to be able to return home to a refrigerator full of food and Christmas presents in the morning. Kelly worried about Elizabeth and asked her father if he thought Mr. Hutchenson would let Elizabeth sleep inside away from the cold night air.

The car disappeared, and Bill stood there alone with Elizabeth. After a minute or so, he opened the trailer door and went back inside.

It was the day after Christmas, and Max was exhausted. He'd preached three morning services to packed crowds at First Church, attended a family party in the afternoon with Kate at a nearby relative's home, and helped serve Christmas dinner at the mission in the evening. All that activity made for one long day, and now he lazily dozed on the couch, his mind finally still from the previous day's ceaseless activity.

Suddenly, the phone rang.

Max debated picking it up. Kate was hitting all the Day-after-Christmas sales with a couple of friends. It was a holiday. Let the answering machine get it.

The answering machine beeped a loud shrill, and a voice came over the line: "Max! If you're there, pick up the phone! It's me, Slade. We've got an emergency! Pick up the . . ."

"Yeah, Slade, I'm here. What is it?"

"Oh, I'm glad you're there. You remember Jake Stone, right? He's one of the guys in our recovery programs. I just received a call from his wife telling me he's using again. She says he drove up to Joshua Tree this morning to go help a buddy with a meth lab. We've got to go get him. He's been in our program for four months. He lost his job last week, and that's probably set him off."

"Slade, where are we going? I don't even know where Joshua Tree is!"

"It's out in the high desert right before the Twenty-Nine Palms Marine Corps base, up above Palm Springs."

"Okay, pick me up in twenty minutes."

Slade and Max sped out the 215 Freeway, connected to Interstate 10, passed the town of Riverside, and drove through the long, dusty San Gorgonio Pass that separates the highest peaks in Southern California—Mt. San Gorgonio to the left and the steep, shadowed slopes of Mt. San Jacinto to the right.

After passing Hadley's Fruit Stand and the monstrous, forty-foot t-rex and brontosaurus dinosaur attractions in the truckstop town of Cabazon, Slade said, "Okay, we're almost at the Sixty-two Freeway. Half an hour and we'll be in Joshua Tree."

During their two-hour journey, Max asked Slade all sorts of questions about the lurid underworld of addiction. Why would someone like Jake up and leave his family and the support of friends and counselors when he seemed to be doing so well in his recovery?

"*Seemed*," Slade slowly said, "that's the operative word. Jake *seemed* to be doing well. Addiction is unlike any other condition known to humanity." Slade curled his fingers around the steering wheel in a slow, rhythmic motion. "Think of it as a huge, voracious octopus of bad choices that wraps one tentacle around your brain and another tentacle around your heart and another one around your spirit . . . another one 'round your family . . . 'nother one 'round your will . . . 'nother one 'round any sense of self-respect you have. Just when you think you've ripped one or two of those things off you, another latches on with thousands of those little suction cups." Slade paused, thinking for a long moment. "It's a beast people fight for the rest of their lives. There's many that break free, but the beast is always there waiting, lurking in the shadows, looking to feed on reckless choices made in moments of fear and panic. Addicts run toward the very things that entangle them. That's what Jake's doing; he's thinking his beast'll rescue him."

Slade went on describing the tyranny of crystal meth addiction and how it seizes its sleepless, frantic adherents like a sudden heart attack. "Crystal methamphetamine," he said, "also known as speed, crank, or meth, is made out of the same ephedrine found in many over-the-counter cold and flu medications, only it's concocted at lethal temperatures with a dangerous mix of toxic chemicals. As a central nervous system stimulant, it's cheaper than crack, one line of its fine powder buying a twelve-hour buzz that's characterized by a feeling of superman-like strength, unceasing work activity, ravenous food binges, nymphomania, hallucinations, and a plethora of other dangerous, high-risk behaviors. Known as a white-trash drug for people trying to hold down a second job, it's also landed its share of workaholic lawyers, doctors, and company executives into the slammer.

"The stuff is like putting anti-freeze on your brain," Slade explained further. "It makes people do crazy, unthinkable things. Paranoia sets in. I knew one guy out of San Diego who spent a whole week whacking on crank; never went to sleep once. Afterward, he shot up a minimart, killed three people. Then blew his own brains out."

Slade shook his head and looked at Max, who was listening and looking out the window at the passing scrub brush and rocky hills.

"What're really bad news are the cookers, the meth labs where they cook the crank. They're like toxic waste dumps. One of those flasks goes off, and the whole town gets rocked by the shock waves."

After passing Yucca Valley, which was near the sparsely populated, sun-baked hamlets of Pioneertown and Flamingo Heights, Slade and Max pulled into Joshua Tree. Like many high desert towns and cities in the adjacent Coachella Valley, Joshua Tree was a tired-looking, lower-class bedroom community, the stepchild to the elegant golf courses, exquisite restaurants, and sparkling pools of nearby Palm Springs and Rancho Mirage. It was the doorway to Joshua Tree National Monument, an incredibly beautiful playground of huge quartz monzanite boulders, awe-inspiring rock formations favored by rock climbers worldwide, and the twisting, spiny, ghostlike trees named by Mormon settlers.

Most of the individuals who lived in Joshua Tree were hardworking people and retirees who loved the simplicity and stillness of desert life but couldn't afford the expensive housing of their wealthier neighbors. But the high desert also had an element—scavenging desert rats, predators in the guise of human flesh—who made their living manufacturing the furies of hell into a powdery white substance.

"How are we going to find him?" Max wondered out loud. "This town's not *that* small. He could be anywhere."

"Nope. When that gong, that craving, starts clanging around in your head, you go straight to the source. Jake's wife, Carla, knew right where Jake was headed. It's an abandoned trailer about five miles out of town. She says this is where Jake always got his stuff before. His friend's a cooker and gives it to him real cheap."

Slade drove through town, passing gas stations, a row of fast-food restaurants, and a few shopping centers. He finally eased his car onto a bumpy dirt road marked by a lone mailbox and a street sign that said Carrion Way.

The two drove for miles looking at the red-flowered ocotillo plants, white jumping cactus, and the occasional roadrunner darting across the road.

Finally, a weathered, silver Gulfstream trailer appeared in the distance, partially hidden by an outcropping of ocher-colored rocks. Slade parked a hundred yards away and told Max they'd walk in from there. Rock music blared from inside the trailer, hopefully making their approach a little less conspicuous.

A dirty, black sedan was parked next to a tan 4 X 4 alongside the trailer. The mesquite-colored window shades were drawn; the puttering whir of a nearby generator was almost drowned out by the intensity of the music.

Twenty yards from the trailer, Slade and Max stopped. Max felt tense, completely out of his element. A bead of sweat rolled down his forehead. Slade looked relaxed, like he knew what he was doing.

"Jake, it's me, Slade! C'mon out! I wanna talk to ya!"

The music stopped. In the window, someone peeked out from behind the shade.

A voice came from inside the trailer, "Go away, Slade. You've got no business being here. I'm busy!"

"Just for a few minutes. Your wife and kids are real worried about you. We're here to help."

"Well, I'm not coming out! You can come in for a minute or so, but not your pastor friend. I only wanna talk with you."

Slade looked at Max and said, "It's probably best you stay here. Who knows what's going on in there? Jake and his friend are probably cooking a batch and don't want any company. I've been in dozens of situations like this before. Crack houses, heroin joints, you name it; I've pulled lots of guys outta abandoned buildings with needles still in their arms. Stay put; I'll be back in a few."

Slade approached the trailer, and the door swung open, revealing the face of a thin, scraggly-faced man Max had never seen before. Slade entered the trailer. The man gave Max a dirty look and quickly slammed the door.

Max stood there with his hands in his pockets, nervously fingering his keys. He could hear the low sound of voices talking back and forth, their words unintelligible. Max prayed for Slade, hoping he could convince Jake to return home with him. He also prayed for Jake, asking God to free him from the chains of addiction.

All of a sudden, there was shouting in the trailer, and seconds later, the sharp burst of a gun. Max froze, not knowing where to go or what to do, fearing shots would start pumping through the window at him. He could hear Slade's voice screaming in anguish, begging, pleading whoever was shooting to stop.

Two more blasts sounded. A fourth shot, a sudden flash, then . . . *ka-boom!* The silver Gulfstream erupted from the inside out. An enormous fireball shot into the cool, blue desert sky, the detonation launching the trailer's contents a hundred feet in the air. The concussive, cataclysmic force burned the flesh of the occupants inside and hurled Max backward onto the hard, rocky ground. A spewing shower of sharp glass and molten shrapnel ripped into Max's face and upper body, leaving him bleeding and unconscious.

The blast blew the generator to pieces, igniting a secondary explosion and spraying fire and gasoline onto the two cars nearby. Engulfed in a swirling fury of flames, the Gulfstream's interior wood siding, plastic fixtures, and fabric cushions were consumed by the fire's voracious hunger. Thick, billowing clouds of black, toxic smoke pealed upward. The intensity of the heat combusted the surrounding tinder-like vegetation. Paint bubbled and popped and spat on each car hood. Soon, all three vehicles were charred hulks consumed in a funeral pyre of destruction and annihilation.

14

Slade Aguilar and Jake Stone were buried the day before New Year's Eve. In a joint memorial service, an overflowing crowd of all colors, races, and backgrounds filled the mission cafeteria with somber faces: the grieving widows, children and immediate family members, friends and relatives of Slade's from San Diego, recovering addicts who were in Jake's program, homeless people, friends from local churches, families from the neighborhood Slade had befriended, high school and college students, and just about everyone involved in the MacArthur Mission effort.

The simple pine caskets sat side by side in the front of the cafeteria. Still recovering from his injuries, Max sat quietly in the second row with Kate. Small cuts and stitches here and there marked the overcast look on his face. Emilio preached a poignant message from John 15:13, "Greater love has no one than this, that one lay down his life for his friends."

"Slade," Emilio tenderly said, "walked in the steps of Jesus all the way. Like Christ, he gave his life for his brother

Jake. Slade asked 'What would Jesus do?' without regard to his personal well-being or comfort or cost. His life, his sacrifice of love, is the ultimate example of bearing the name of Christ. He was my friend, he was Jake's friend, he was your friend . . . *he was God's friend.*"

When Emilio was finished, Rikki stood and sang a beautiful hymn in Spanish that left everyone in tears. The fluid, resonating sound of her voice and the stirring melody merged to touch every soul in a way that was impossible with mere words. After her song, family and friends eulogized the two dead men for thirty minutes. Remarkably, no one glossed over the realities of addiction and its ultimate costs. There was nothing to celebrate about the senseless deaths of two men who were loved by their families and friends. The whole service was a cacophony of conflicting emotions. At one level, there was intense grief and loss. At another, hope and faith.

The memorial service ended and a reception was held immediately afterward. A little while later, the families of the deceased left for private graveside services at two different cemeteries in the L.A. area.

New Year's Day came, and once again the California sun shone a pleasant sixty-nine degrees as over a million people lined the streets of Pasadena for the annual Tournament of Roses parade. Dragons with smoking nostrils chased damsels in distress. Roaring tigers jumped through flaming hoops. Dinosaurs danced in a rock and roll band. One-hundred-piece marching bands dressed in their finest parade dress. Arabian equestrian teams were decked out in shimmering silver. The extravagant display of motorized floats decorated in rose petals, palm leaves, yellow mums, purple daisies, corn husks, hydrangea, coffee grounds, carnations, irises, day lilies, seaweed, and thousands of other types of plants and vegetation held waving princesses, movie stars, and laughing children.

Max stayed home and watched the parade on television with Kate, Vic Gennaro and his wife, June, and Sam Baker. He was physically present, but his mind was at the movies, replaying over and over the events of the final day he had spent with Slade. Slade and Jake were dead. He could have been killed too!

Watching the Rose Bowl game itself was out of the question. Max was still sore from the blast and couldn't hear out of one ear. The emergency room doctors had told him he was fortunate to be alive.

After a restful nap in the afternoon, Max went up to his study and began the difficult task of preparing his Sunday message. Though his body ached and his medication left him feeling drowsy, his mind was clear. He felt a deep stirring in his heart and was compelled to write down his thoughts. When he was done, he went downstairs and had a long talk with Kate over coffee and his favorite chocolate chip cookies. Then, Max called Emilio.

On Sunday morning, the winter sun crept slowly over the snow-covered peaks of Mt. Baldy and, in a few hours, First Church was filled like never before. Max slowly rose to the pulpit and began reading the story of the young man who came to Jesus, asking him what he must do to obtain eternal life. He read Jesus' words to him: "Sell all that you have and give it to the poor and you will have treasure in heaven; and then, come follow me." Max noted that the young man was not willing to suffer for Jesus in that way. Then he voiced the difficult question that some of his congregants had likely been asking themselves: If following Jesus means suffering so much, isn't there an easier way?

"This has been a tremendously difficult week for me as well as for many of you who are mourning the deaths of Slade Aguilar and Jake Stone. I want to personally thank you for all the supportive letters, phone calls, flowers, and encouragement I've received. We began last January with the death of Jack Manning, and here we are, a year later, grieving two more unexpected deaths. I don't know about you, but I don't feel my heart can be broken into any smaller pieces than it is now.

"A lot has happened this past year, and it all began with one homeless man asking 'What would Jesus do?' Countless lives have been changed, many of yours included, by that one simple question. Two weeks from now will mark the one-year anniversary of the promise I proposed. I could go on and on telling you how proud I am of you and what a privilege it is to be your pastor, but right now the words of Jesus call us to consider this important story. We'll have a celebration in a few weeks, but let's pause to reflect on the implications of what it truly means to follow in the steps of Christ.

"Is it true," Max then asked in a quiet, reflective voice, "that the church of today, the church that is called after Christ's own name, would refuse to follow him to avoid suffering and physical loss? Does the church contain men and women who think more about their own ease—their next home, their next new car, next vacation or retirement fund—than of the sufferings and needs and sins of humanity? Are the Christians of America ready to have their discipleship tested? How about the men and women of great wealth? Are they ready to take their wealth and use it as Jesus would? How about the men and women of great talent? Are they ready to give their gifts and abilities to be used for the kingdom of God?"

No one in the congregation moved. All eyes were forward, heads and shoulders leaning ahead to hear these piercing words spoken with passion and clarity.

Max Henry had always had a dramatic preaching style, but ever since he promised to do as Jesus would do, his *life* had become his message. Everyone seated at First Church this morning felt the authentic sincerity and humble compassion of a man who had gone deep into this truth, as if it had been driven through his heart with a wooden stake.

"What is the test of following Christ? Is it not the same today as it was in Jesus' time? Have our culture, our surroundings, our wants and desires, modified or changed the test? Are our actions and lifestyles dictated by the subtle siren song of the media, the ups and downs of the marketplace, the conflicts in our marriages and relationships, the prison chains of materialism, or the whims of our inherently selfish nature? If Jesus were here today, would he not call some of the members of this very church to do just as he commanded the rich young man, and ask them to give up their wealth and literally follow him? If any church member, any person who calls themselves 'Christian,' loved his or her possessions more than the Savior, I believe Christ would call them to do the same. The test would be the same today as then.

"I have seen amazing things happen this past year at First Church and the MacArthur Park Mission. So have you. Many of you have put your faith to the test by being faithful to the promise to ask 'What would Jesus do?' I am awed by the sacrifices you have made in your personal and professional lives. It is only as a fellow follower and brother in Christ that I can preach this message. Several of you have made greater sacrifices than I, and you could full well stand at this podium today and speak this message in integrity and love. But so be it that God has given me the grace to do so, let my words be spoken with the humility of Christ.

"We hear message after message of God's love and grace, but is the gospel message any less today than it was two thousand years ago when Christ said, 'If anyone would come after me, he must deny himself and take up the cross daily and follow me. For whoever wants to save his life will lose it, but whoever loses his life for me will save it'? What would Jesus do in our city and in every city across America? What would he do about the homeless, the hungry, the unemployed, the addicted, the elderly, the sick, the lonely, the orphan, the prisoner, the prostitute, the beggar, and the broken?

"Does the church fulfill its heavenly calling in following Jesus when it gives so little money to missions or eradicating the extreme cases of poverty in our society? Is it any sacrifice for a man who is worth ten million dollars to give ten thousand dollars for the poor and the hungry? Isn't he giving something that costs him practically nothing so far as any personal pain or suffering goes? Is it true that the followers of Christ today in most of our churches are living soft, selfish lives, very far from any sacrifice that can be called sacrifice? What would Jesus do?

"If our definition of being a Christian is simply to enjoy the privileges of worship, insulating ourselves with other believers from the traumas of this world, being generous at no real expense to ourselves, having a good, easy time surrounded by comfortable pleasures, and at the same time avoid the great stress of sin and hardship of this earth because it is too painful—if this is our definition of Christianity—then surely we are a long way from following the steps of Christ, who cried from the cross of Calvary, 'My God! My God! Why have you forsaken me'!"

When Max finished his sermon, a great hush, like the settling of leaves after a sudden wind, came over the audience. Everyone thought he was finished, but he began again.

"It is these words, the very words of Christ that have moved so deeply in my heart this week. The deaths of Slade and Jake, and also the death of Jack Manning a year ago this month, have riveted my attention to what really matters in this life. I have discovered that what really matters is following Jesus wholeheartedly, regardless of the cost, regardless of the circumstances. To go where he leads is my mission in life, and it is with this conviction that I must say . . ."

Max hesitated, the emotional tone of his voice drawing everyone's rapt attention. People wondered where he was leading, what he was going to say next; what was he alluding to?

"There is a new and unexpected opening for the directorship of the MacArthur Mission. A few days ago, I spoke with Emilio Alvarez, our elder board, and the mission foundation directors about my future, and I have concluded that the Lord is leading me a few miles west of here. This is something I've been thinking and praying about long before the deaths of our two friends. Effective February 1, next month, I will step down from my position here at First Church and will begin working immediately as the director of the MacArthur Mission. It's with great sadness that Kate and I will be leaving First Church, but I am also very excited to be able to build on the important work started by Slade and his team."

No one in the congregation said a word as Max left the pulpit and the choir rose to sing a final anthem. Some wondered if what they'd just heard was correct. *Max Henry leave First Church?*

When these individuals saw that many to their right and left had the same surprised reaction, they began visibly shaking their heads as if not wanting to admit to the truth of what they'd just heard. After that, for a long moment, no one moved or said anything.

Then, in the back of the sanctuary, a few people began to slowly clap. As others caught on, especially those who had been a part of the fellowship hall gathering, the clapping began to build. This swell of love and support grew louder and louder as the people of First Church realized that Max Henry's decision was the direct result of following Jesus wherever he led. The applause surged and leaped from aisle to aisle like a sailboat slicing through churning breakers on a windy sea. Soon the energetic and appreciative applause thundered into a deafening roar of hearty cheers and ear-piercing whistles.

Max stood, waved, and thanked everyone. He motioned toward the choir director, and the service closed with a song of praise to God.

Later that afternoon, Max left his house, hopped on his Harley, and headed out of Pasadena. He went north on the 210 Freeway, past La Canada-Flintridge, and connected to the 2, the old Angeles Crest Highway. Cruising through the winding mountain road, he throttled the Harley higher and higher above the Los Angeles basin. It was a beautiful January day. Clear. Crisp. Wind wasn't too cold. A perfect day for riding.

Snaking up the mountainside, passing manzanita trees with their vermilion bark and fragrant pine trees, Max thought about the events of the past year and the miraculous things God had done. He began to dream about what could happen to every church in America if Christians were willing to go with Jesus all the way. He saw a new vision of the bride of Christ alive and awake, ready to meet her king.

He saw more churches and individuals getting involved in the mission effort, eager to serve the poor and the homeless. He saw Kate and himself ministering to the needy and addicted in the rough neighborhoods of downtown Los Angeles. He saw the two of them living simpler lifestyles, content with what they had, rearranging their lifestyle as needed.

He saw Rikki Winslow continuing to use her singing gifts with the children and families of the mission. Rikki's voice, along with her heart yielded to God, would continue to inspire, drawing the weak and the weary to the arms of

Christ. Perhaps there could be a wedding, in the future of course, between her and Brock. They'd been dating the past few months and there was no telling where that might lead.

Brock. Max remembered the first day he met him at Starbucks. He had been cocky and self-assured at first, but since he had given himself to God, Brock had become kinder, humbler, and willing to consider others before himself. Max saw Brock growing in his capacity to love and give, using his enormous resources for the betterment of humankind.

He saw Gina Page increasing in her devotion to the Lord and love for others. A generous spirit, Gina would be fulfilled by living a life of purposeful activity and not squandering her wealth on the indulgences of youth. She, along with Rikki, would continue to play a pivotal role in the mission's growth and development. Her energy and enthusiasm were contagious; her willingness to sacrifice sincere.

He saw Alex Powers continuing to excel with his intellectual gifts and computer prowess. His stint at PowerNet was but a test. Alex's faithfulness to God and his commitment to holiness were small seeds that would eventually sprout into harvests of greatness in the coming years of his life. He may have given up his stock options, but what was revealed was an inner value no one could ever buy.

With their vigorous life experience and wisdom, innovative employee programs, and willingness to mentor younger men, Sam Baker and Vic Gennaro would live long lives saturated with meaning and significance. They would serve as role models to other older men and women on how to prepare for their heavenly home by leaving earth with a legacy of love.

Like any family with teenagers, Max saw the Matthews family weathering their seasons of conflict with strength and determination, albeit with some moments of to-be-expected madness. Though they might continue to struggle financially, David and Jessica would deepen their commitment to one another and provide their children the richest example possible of God's love and grace.

He saw Paul Wickman, broken from the severing of divorce, but at the same time, still hopeful and dependent on Christ. In the future, Paul would have ample opportunity to show the movers and shakers of the financial world the dependable confidence he discovered.

There too was Candice Sterling and her little bundle of Hope. Max saw her facing the challenges of being a single mother with courage and optimism. There would be difficult days ahead, but Candice was a talented young woman surrounded by the support of family and friends.

And finally, Max saw Don Marsh maturing to be a man of purpose and responsibility. His commitment to Christ was still as fresh as the celebration of Christmas, but through months of encouragement from Sam, Brock, Rikki, and Gina, Don's demeanor had transformed from glum despair to a sense of anticipation and hope about his future. Max saw Don being groomed for an opportunity to be revealed by Sam in the coming years, but only when Don was ready.

He also saw Don riding a Harley. His Harley. A week earlier, Don's old car had finally given up the ghost with a cracked engine block on the 210 Freeway. Max talked about it with Kate and figured why not. Don didn't have enough money for a decent used car, and Max didn't ride the bike much anyway. He couldn't wait to surprise him.

As Max neared the Mt. Wilson observatory, the great expanse of the largest city on the West Coast lay before him. In the distance, the setting sun bathed the city in warm, waning rays from past the Palos Verdes Peninsula.

Los Angeles: a study in contrasts. A land of movie stars and homeless beggars. Rodeo Drive and Skid Row. Capital Records and crack cocaine. Rock 'n' roll and rejection. Hollywood and halfway houses. Dodger Dogs and hungry children. Rose parades and the pornography industry. Theme restaurants and immigrant labor. Beach-front mansions and misery. Wealth and grandeur. Desperation and hopelessness. As he looked at the magnificence below him, Max couldn't help but wonder what Christ felt when Satan was tempting him in the desert as he was shown the kingdoms of the world and all their splendor. All could have been his if he had only bowed down and worshipped a master that was not his own.

Max looked above and past the city to the fading sun and cried in his heart, "Lord, teach me to follow! Your kingdom come, your will be done! Bring your light to dawn on your church, and wake us fresh to serve you every day. Help us to bring your truth and your love to the world below. Show us how to bring the church to you 'without spot or wrinkle.' Help us to be obedient, following you all the way."

The sun burned into the Pacific, the last vestiges of light scattered in hazy celadon and indigo hues tinted on the clouds above.

It'd be dark soon. Max turned the Harley around and headed back down the hill, steeled in his resolve to keep the promise, ready to follow in his steps.